"Do you want me as much as I want you, Vanessa?" Linc asked, his lips poised tantalizingly above hers.

No woman had ever had this wild, explosive effect on him. When he took her in his arms, the careful, controlled man he knew himself to be was transformed into a passionate, sensual man. His hands roamed over her possessively, arousingly. He knew she was as hungry for him as he was for her, and he wanted to hear her say it. He *needed* to hear her say it.

He nipped teasingly at her lips and she protested the sensual torment with a soft moan. "Say it, Vanessa."

Vanessa quivered. He sounded sexy, and commanding, and very male, and she forgot that she was Vanessa Ramsey, whom no man dared to command. She forgot he was totally unsuitable for her in every way. "Yes, Linc," she breathed in a soft, sexy, feminine voice she scarcely recognized as her own. "I want you."

And then his mouth was on hers and she felt fireworks explode in her head. . . .

WHAT ARE *LOVESWEPT* ROMANCES?

They are stories of true romance and touching emotion. We believe those two very important ingredients are constants in our highly sensual and very believable stories in the *LOVESWEPT* line. Our goal is to give you, the reader, stories of consistently high quality that may sometimes make you laugh, sometimes make you cry, but are always fresh and creative and contain many delightful surprises within their pages.

Most romance fans read an enormous number of books. Those they truly love, they keep. Others may be traded with friends and soon forgotten. We hope that each *LOVESWEPT* romance will be a treasure—a "keeper." We will always try to publish

LOVE STORIES YOU'LL NEVER FORGET
BY AUTHORS YOU'LL ALWAYS REMEMBER

The Editors

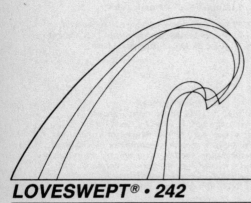

LOVESWEPT® • 242

Barbara Boswell
Intimate Details

BANTAM BOOKS
TORONTO • NEW YORK • LONDON • SYDNEY • AUCKLAND

INTIMATE DETAILS
A Bantam Book / March 1988

LOVESWEPT® and the wave device are registered
trademarks of Bantam Books. Registered in U.S. Patent
and Trademark Office and elsewhere.

If you would be interested in receiving protective vinyl
covers for your Loveswept books, please write to this address
for information:

Loveswept
Bantam Books
P.O. Box 985
Hicksville, NY 11802

ISBN 0-553-21883-2

Published simultaneously in the United States and Canada

Bantam Books are published by Bantam Books, a division
of Bantam Doubleday Dell Publishing Group, Inc. Its trademark, consisting of the words "Bantam Books" and the
portrayal of a rooster, is Registered in U.S. Patent and
Trademark Office and in other countries. Marca Registrada.
Bantam Books, 666 Fifth Avenue, New York, New York 10103.

Prologue

"Mr Ramsey, Edward Templeton is on line one." The voice of Quentin Ramsey's private secretary came over the office intercom, interrupting the meeting between Quentin and his daughter, Vanessa.

Vanessa thought her father looked rather relieved at the intrusion. "You run along now, princess," he said, reaching for the phone. "Take a nice, long lunch and then spend the rest of the afternoon shopping. Buy yourself a pretty dress for the party tonight, hmm?"

"I don't need another dress, Daddy. What I need is for you to—"

"Bye-bye, kitten." He blew her a kiss as he turned his full attention to the caller on the phone. It was a visible, observable transformation when Quentin Ramsey switched from his role of doting father to his role as chairman of the board of Ramsey & Sons Development Corporation, the privately owned family company which built, developed, and managed shopping malls and office complexes in thirty states.

Vanessa realized the futility of trying to continue their discussion. She stormed out of her father's luxurious corner office and flew down the hall to the opposite end of the corridor and the almost equally sumptuous corner office of her eldest brother Rad, president of Ramsey & Sons.

She marched past his secretary who, wisely, made

no effort to stop her. "I have to talk to you!" she announced to her brother, who put down the file he was reading and looked up.

Rad arched his brows. "Uh-oh. Let me guess Another run-in with Dad?"

" 'Bye-bye, kitten,' he says! 'Run along, princess,' he says!" Vanessa fumed. "As if I were three years old!"

"You're Daddy's Little Girl," Rad said with a shrug. "So what else is new?"

"Nothing is new." Vanessa paced the office like a sleek, caged cat. "Nothing is ever new when it comes to Daddy, Mama, and me. I'll always be their vapid little nitwit with her imbecilic window-dressing job. Ramsey and *Sons*, that says it all, Rad. I'm their daughter and there's no place for me in this organization!"

"What happened this time, Vanessa?" Rad asked patiently with a touch of older brother condescension that Vanessa noted but did not remark upon. Rad was the only one of her four brothers who seriously acknowledged her frustration with her specially created non-job at Ramsey & Sons. Slade, her second oldest brother and an executive vice-president with the company, still viewed her as his kid sister, the party girl. Jed, the next brother in line and another vice-president, mocked her ambitions as a frivolous whim. Ricky, five years younger than she, was still in college. But there would be a responsible, interesting, and challenging position for him in the company upon his graduation, she knew. He wouldn't be stuck in a cute little office decorated in shades of pink and urged to spend his days shopping and lunching with other bored society girls.

Vanessa took a deep breath. "Rad, I tried to show Daddy my designs for the interior of the new Consolidated office building and shopping center we're building in Pittsburgh. You know the trouble we've been having with the space planners on that one, and I have exactly what the clients want." She tossed a thick portfolio onto Rad's desk. "But Daddy won't even look at it. He's adamant about sticking with the space planners we've already retained."

"You know how Dad feels about corporate loyalty, Vanessa."

"But my designs are better, Rad. I've seen their plans for this building, and mine are more efficient and innovative. I'm good at space planning, Rad, you've admitted it yourself every time you've looked at my work. And you know that I did so well in my design and space planning classes in college that I won that nationally sponsored contest and was offered a job by three of the leading architectural firms in New York City!"

Rad sighed. "I know, Vanessa. And I know how crushed you were when you had to turn them all down and stay here in Houston."

She rolled her eyes. "The folks nearly went crazy when I suggested moving to New York. They couldn't even handle the thought of me living alone in Dallas."

"I remember." Rad nodded, his gray eyes revealing a mixture of sympathy and exasperation. "Mother wept around the clock and Dad insisted that you were driving his blood pressure so high, he was going to drop dead at any given moment. And then you gave in to them and agreed to live at home and accept the job of creative consultant—whatever that is—with Ramsey & Sons, and Mom was all smiles again and Dad's blood pressure was miraculously restored to normal levels."

"Rad, why won't Dad give me a chance?" she asked for perhaps the thousandth time. "I've done designs for every single project since I started working here three years ago, and he refuses even to glance at them. The company needs what I'm good at doing, what I love to do. Why have I been forced into this frivolous, superfluous role?"

"Because Dad can't handle the idea of his precious little daughter doing what he considers *men's work*," Rad said dryly. "Horrors! That's not what the Ramsey

Crown Princess was born and bred to do. You weren't supposed to do so well in college, Vanessa. You were supposed to skate by with barely passing grades while you socialized and looked for a husband. You weren't supposed to be talented and ambitious and competitive. You were just supposed to be pretty and make yourself a good match. However . . ."

"Yes, their plans for me seen to have gone somewhat awry." Vanessa's gray eyes gleamed wickedly and she cast Rad a sudden devilish smile. "I may be stuck living at home and playing at a pretend job, but much to Mama and Daddy's despair I still haven't settled down with an acceptable, respectable young man and produced the requisite Ramsey grandchildren."

Rad grinned. "No, indeed. The society deb has turned into an outspoken, unpredictable terror whom half the men in Houston are scared to death of."

"And the other half hope to marry for money." Vanessa shook her head and grimaced. Her eyes flicked to the photograph of Rad's family proudly displayed on his desk. "Don't you ever try to force your girls into this kind of straitjacket existence, Rad Ramsey. Because if you do, old Aunt Vanessa will personally come to their rescue."

Rad picked up the picture. His wife, Erin, preschoolers Carrie Beth and Courtney, and baby son Connor smiled up at him. "You have no worries on that score, Vanessa. Erin and I plan to give all our kids the freedom to live their own lives."

"Lucky them." Vanessa sighed. "Well, look over my designs, will you? Not that I have any hopes that you'll be able to convince Daddy to make use of them. I already have my assignment for the day—lunch and shopping." She frowned. "Jack and Coralie Wallace's party is tonight at the club. I don't suppose you and Erin are going?"

Rad shook his head. "We're not on the party circuit, Vanessa."

"There are many times when I wish I weren't. I

guess Slade and Shavonne won't be there either?" Slade's wife Shavonne was Erin's sister. Their daughter Robin was an energetic, tow-headed toddler.

"No, I doubt it. So it'll be up to you to represent the Ramseys in your usual inimitable style."

"Oh, Rad, I'm so bored with the same old parties and the same old people! And I'm bored to tears with my silly job that isn't a job at all! Sometimes I feel as if I'm drowning and going down for the third time. I get so damn frustrated."

"It can't be easy, but don't give up hope, little sis." Rad placed a brotherly hand on her shoulder. "I'll try to talk to Dad again on your behalf."

"And it'll do as much good as it's done before," she said gloomily. "But thanks anyway, Rad."

He watched her walk out of the office, then picked up the portfolio. A half hour later, he buzzed his father's office. "Dad, I think you ought to look over Vanessa's space plans for the Consolidated Building. They're—"

"So she's been badgering you, too?" Quentin's voice held exasperated indulgence. "Little Vanessa and her drawings!"

"Dad, Vanessa is unhappy and frustrated and—"

"I know, Rad. And it pains me and your mama to see our little kitten unhappy."

"Dad, Vanessa is nobody's little kitten. She's a headstrong and impetuous woman. She's willful and reckless and completely bored with her life. I view her as a timebomb waiting to explode."

"I agree with you," Quentin said slowly. "And that's why I've taken the necessary steps to ensure her happiness—as well as her safety and well-being."

"Uh-oh." Rad ran a hand through his hair. "Why do I know that whatever Machiavellian scheme you've cooked up has nothing to do with Vanessa's ability in space planning and interior design?"

"Son, tonight Vanessa is going to meet the man who is going to change her life and give it some direction and meaning."

Rad groaned. "Not another matchmaking attempt? Dad, give the girl a break!"

"Rad, your little sister will thank me for this a year from now when she's a contented wife and mother."

"Is that the theme song for *Father Knows Best* I hear playing in the background?"

Quentin chuckled. "Try 'Some Enchanted Evening'—because that's exactly what it's going to be for our little princess."

One

"That's him, Vanessa. The tall, blond hunk talking to Lexie Madison." Melinda Sue Harper directed her gaze toward the fair-haired man who appeared deeply engrossed in conversation with a striking redhead. They were all gathered in one of the large, formally elegant private party rooms at the River Oaks Country Club. "He's the one who asked Coralie to let him know the moment you arrived. He wants to be introduced to you."

Vanessa glanced at the stranger. He was almost an inch under six feet, she noted critically. Her father and brothers were all at least an inch or two over six feet. "He's short," she said dismissively.

"He is not," argued Melinda Sue. "You're wearing three-and-a-half-inch heels and he's still taller than you are."

"But only a couple inches taller. I like a man to tower over me. And, anyway, he's blond." Her father and brothers all had dark hair, as she did. "I'm not interested in blonds."

"You were mighty interested in Troy Timmons and he's blond," Melinda Sue said slyly.

Vanessa inclined her chin to a regal tilt. "Troy is just a good friend. When I saw him last month in New York, I met some of his new friends and we all had a lovely time together." Her light gray eyes glittered with challenge, and Melinda Sue immediately backed off. Most people did when confronted by the full force of a Ramsey stare.

"But you have to admit that you've occasionally broken your tall, dark, and handsome rule and gone out with blond guys," Melinda Sue pointed out, returning to their original topic of discussion. She cast an admiring glance at the blond stranger and sighed. "Take a good look at him, Vanessa. He's gorgeous! Every woman at this party has been drooling over him since he arrived, including me. But he specifically requested to be introduced to you!"

Vanessa frowned. "Look at his clothes, Mindy. His suit and tie are strictly bargain basement. I'll wager his shirt and shoes are, too."

"So he doesn't dress in designer labels. Don't be such a snob, Vanessa. His clothes may not cost much, but he sure wears them well. Look at those shoulders of his!"

"Melinda Sue, I'm not being a snob, I'm being a realist. I've learned to spot men who are bent on using me to advance themselves. Do you have any idea how many men I meet who view me as their ticket to an executive position in my father's company with an unlimited expense account, to custom-tailored clothing and a sports car? That man is one of them, I can tell. He's a fortune hunter. That's the only reason he wants to meet me."

"The only reason? Come on, Vanessa, it's not like you to be modest. I've watched guys flock around you since we were in the eighth grade. You're gorgeous, girl. That's why that dreamy guy wants to meet you. And I must say, you two would make a stunning couple."

"You're an incorrigible romantic, Mindy," Vanessa said dryly. "Fortunately, I'm not or I would have been married years ago by a man who wanted my family's money."

Melinda Sue looked thoughtful. "A man with his looks doesn't have to be a fortune hunter, Vanessa. He can get any woman he wants."

"Mindy, honey, all fortune hunters are good-looking," Vanessa explained patiently. "Looks are their stock-in-trade. And the only women they want are rich ones. I've been fending off fortune hunters since I turned seventeen. I'm quite familiar with the species and, believe me—their place in the animal kingdom is somewhere near reptiles."

Melinda Sue continued to eye the handsome blond man rather longingly. "Well, Lexie Madison certainly seems taken with him. She looks like she's hanging on his every word."

"They ought to get on well, they're both gold diggers. You know what they say about birds of a feather . . ." Vanessa surveyed the pair coolly, then her gaze flicked to the other side of the room. "Mindy, I must go over and say hello to Paul and Terese McDonald. I'll talk to you later."

She was threading her way through the crowd when Coralie Wallace, the hostess of the party, caught her arm. "Vanessa, there's someone who would like to meet you and I promised that I'd—"

"Make the introductions," Vanessa finished for her. "Never mind, Coralie, introduce him to Melinda Sue instead. She's panting to meet him."

"But, Vanessa, I have to introduce him to *you*," Coralie said nervously.

Vanessa paused to stare sharply at Coralie, and her gray eyes narrowed shrewdly. "Why do you have to introduce him to me, Coralie?"

Coralie managed a wan smile. "Well, I—uh—he—that is—your—" She ceased stammering and suddenly smiled in obvious relief. Vanessa whirled around to see the blond stranger approaching them. Coralie rushed forward to take his arm and fairly drag him to Vanessa's side.

"Vanessa, this is Lincoln Scott. Linc, meet Vanessa Ramsey," Coralie said without pausing to breathe. Having performed the introductions, she hurried off, citing her hostess duties as an excuse.

Vanessa's gaze flicked over Lincoln Scott. Her first

thought was that Melinda Sue Harper was right. The man was gorgeous. The acknowledgment irritated her greatly. But his sun-streaked blond hair, his deep blue eyes fringed with thick, dark lashes, and his well-proportioned muscular frame would earn him an eleven on the proverbial one-to-ten ratings scale.

Vanessa drew in a sharp breath. She was appalled that her heart had skipped a beat, that her mouth was suddenly dry. Her involuntary feminine response to the man was both annoying and disconcerting. She sought to deny it by denying his physical appeal. His hair was cut shorter than she liked, she thought, his nose was too straight, his mouth too—she immediately looked away. His mouth was perfect, there was no way around that. Instead, she zeroed in on his jaw which she decided was too strong for her liking.

And then there was the matter of height. He might be just shy of six feet, but she still had to look up at him. It irked her, particularly when his dark blue eyes met hers.

Vanessa held his gaze; she wasn't about to be the first to look away.

"So you're Vanessa Ramsey," he said.

He had a gravelly, husky voice which flowed over her like hot honey. She almost responded with a reflexive polite smile and nod. Almost. She caught herself just in time. "Yes, I am," she replied frostily.

His blue eyes seemed to be locked with hers. Vanessa wished he would drop his gaze, so she could look away. But he didn't, and of course, she wouldn't.

He said nothing, which surprised her. Fortune-hunting charm boys generally had a smooth line of patter designed to ingratiate themselves with their targets. She waited for the winning smile that he would undoubtedly flash as he spouted his rehearsed-to-dazzle introduction.

But Lincoln Scott didn't smile. It occurred to Vanessa that he hadn't smiled once since Coralie's hasty introduction. That surprised her, too. Usually, these eager-to-romance-her-and-get-rich charmers were always flashing toothpaste-ad grins and boyish dimples.

He cleared his throat and glanced at the dance band which had begun to play a slow song. Several couples were already dancing. "Uh, would you like to dance?"

Vanessa stared at him. He seemed almost nervous as he asked, totally unlike the golden-voiced smoothies she knew so well. This poor sucker had a long way to go in the rich-wife market, she decided. He must be a newcomer to the field.

"No, I don't care to dance," she replied succinctly, pleased that he had been the first to look away. She loved winning, even the most minor skirmish. She gave her head a toss and her thick, chestnut-burnished hair cascaded over her shoulders. "If you'll excuse me, Mr. Scott, I see some friends—"

"Vanessa, I have to talk with you."

She stopped in her tracks and turned to stare at him. His tone was unmistakably . . . commanding? She drew herself up to her full height, an impressive five-foot-nine with the supplementing air of her three-and-a-half-inch heels. It was annoying that he was still a couple of inches taller than she, but she compensated by shooting him a look that would surely freeze fire. "Mr. Scott, I have nothing to say to you," she told him in the imperious manner of a royal empress, born to rule. "And may I suggest that you do yourself a favor and set your fortune-hunting sights on someone else. You'll only be wasting your time with me."

She swept grandly away from him, and was promptly intercepted by Melinda Sue who fired a barrage of questions at her. "What did he say? What did he want? Who is he?"

"His name is Lincoln Scott, and he said nothing worth quoting," Vanessa replied.

Melinda Sue looked disappointed. But only for a

moment. "I was talking to Lexie about him and she said he asked her all sorts of questions about you, Vanessa. And do you know what she told him?" Melinda Sue assumed an affronted expression, but her eyes gleamed with enthusiasm. "She said you were the biggest balls-buster in the state of Texas!"

Lincoln Scott chose that moment to join them. Melinda Sue blushed. Vanessa scowled at him. "I understand you and Lexie Madison have been gossiping about me, Mr. Scott," she said icily.

Melinda Sue's flush deepened to scarlet. "Oh, Vanessa!" She groaned.

Lincoln Scott appeared equally discomfited by Vanessa's blunt accusation. "I wasn't gossiping about you, Vanessa. Lexie Madison introduced herself to me two minutes after I arrived at the party. I asked her if she knew Vanessa Ramsey and she said that she did."

"And then you proceeded to listen to her gleefully rip me apart."

"Now that you mention it, she was fairly gleeful about it," Linc said thoughtfully. "But don't worry, I took everything she said with the proverbial grain of salt."

"That certainly spares me a lot of sleepless nights," Vanessa snapped.

"Good." He smiled, his first smile of the evening.

Vanessa felt her heart stop—the effect of his smile was that potent. Uh-oh, she thought, and immediately took a step backward. When the smile of a fortune hunter packed that much of a wallop, it was time to absent herself. "Mr. Scott wants to dance, Mindy," she called as she glided away from them. "Why don't you show him how?"

Linc and Melinda Sue faced each other. "I think I struck out," he said glumly.

"Oh, well, you're probably better off." Melinda Sue shrugged, then smiled cheerfully. "Vanessa is one of my oldest and dearest friends, but I'm afraid what Lexie Madison said about her is true. She's managed to, uh, neuter a lot of guys."

"I'm going to marry her," Linc said.

"Lexie Madison?"

"Vanessa Ramsey."

Mindy laughed. "How do you intend to pull that off without divine intervention? She won't even dance with you! She thinks you're a fortune-hunting creep."

"I'm not." He frowned. "Not exactly."

Melinda Sue giggled. "Well, you've got your work cut out for you, honey. Vanessa's used to men chasing her, she's used to men throwing themselves at her feet. But the only man she ever really seemed interested in turned out to be"—she glanced around quickly and lowered her voice—"gay!"

Linc grimaced and said nothing, but his silence did not deter Melinda Sue. "Troy Timmons, that's the guy's name, lives in New York now and Vanessa maintains a friendship with him. A purely platonic one, of course. I guess it just goes to show that money can't buy happiness," she added gaily. "Oops! Wrong thing to say to a fortune hunter. Good luck with Vanessa. You're going to need it."

Linc watched her walk away to join a group gathered nearby. A few moments later, they were casting amused, speculative glances at him, and he knew that Melinda Sue was merrily telling all. With an inward groan, he made his way through the crowd, searching for Vanessa.

Sweep her off her feet, Lincoln, my boy. The voice of Quentin Ramsey, Vanessa's father, echoed in his head, mocking him. It was impossible to sweep a woman off her feet when one was tongue-tied in her presence, he thought. Vanessa Ramsey was accustomed to being charmed by the suave and the smooth. He must have appeared a complete dolt. He certainly felt like one.

He spotted Vanessa on the dance floor with a lithe and handsome partner, matching intricate steps with seemingly effortless grace and precision. Staring at her, he felt it again, the same fist-in-the-gut sensation that had robbed him of speech—not to mention thought and breath—when Quentin Ramsey had shown him the pictures of Vanessa yesterday. He'd felt it again tonight when he'd first seen her in the flesh. It had doubled in intensity when they'd been introduced. He truly understood the phrase "struck dumb" because he had been, then and now.

His gaze traveled over her, taking in her long, rich mane of dark hair, her high cheekbones and mesmerizing, wide-set clear gray eyes. Her features were nothing short of perfection, and her hyacinth blue silk dress—which he guessed cost more than the three suits he owned—elegantly accentuated the curves of her figure. The skirt was tight with a long slit up the side and the two tiny straps were more decorative than functional in holding up the bodice that lovingly hugged her breasts. She had a model's body, he noted, small breasts, narrow waist, and slim hips. Her legs were long and shapely, her ankles slender.

The photographs her father had shown him did not really do her justice, though, Linc thought dazedly. They were merely one-dimensional images of a beautiful woman. In person Vanessa projected a glowing, vibrant magnetism that no film could capture. He felt his body tighten as a tidal wave of desire welled up within him. It was more than a little alarming, for no woman had ever stirred such a strong, primitive response to him.

Vanessa was not unaware of her audience. She was used to admiring stares; she'd been a beautiful child who'd grown into a beautiful woman, and admiring stares came with the territory. Usually, she accepted the silent admiration while ignoring it. But she couldn't seem to ignore Lincoln Scott. She wasn't sure why she had even noticed him watching her, and she had no idea why her eyes kept sliding to him to see if he was still watching her.

He was. Once, her gaze lingered a bit too long, and he smiled and nodded to her, acknowledging her stare. Vanessa quickly looked away, feeling irritated. He wasn't supposed to have done that. She turned her full concentration on her dancing and her partner and when she looked up again, Lincoln Scott was gone.

"May I cut in?"

She started at the sound of the gravelly male voice. Lincoln Scott had come up behind her. Her partner, Jay Travis, frowned. "I really don't think—" he began.

Linc didn't give him time to finish. He inserted himself in front of Vanessa and took her hand. She gave him a long-suffering glance, then turned to her former partner. "It's all right, Jay, I'll dance with Mr. Scott. Just this one time," she added coolly.

He held her at a respectful distance as he began a methodical box step. Vanessa wondered if he was counting to himself, for he didn't say a word to her. She was unaccustomed to silence from a man. Every man she'd ever met had talked a blue streak in an effort to impress her.

Melinda Sue and Jay danced by. Mindy grinned and waved, then stood on tiptoe to whisper something in Jay's ear. He made an obvious show of gaping incredulously from Vanessa to Lincoln, then let out a raucous burst of laughter.

Vanessa began to burn. Jay was an excellent dancer and quite vain about his skill. She was certain that his nose was out of joint because Lincoln had cut in on them and was now making disparaging remarks about his pitiful box step.

"Just ignore them," she advised Linc. "And don't lose count." She didn't know why she felt protective of him. He was twice as muscular as the reed-thin Jay.

With commendable agility, she moved her foot just as Linc missed a step. "Sorry," he murmured.

"It's all right."

Jay was still laughing, and Melinda Sue had joined in. Vanessa cast them a killing glance as Linc nearly trod on her toe again. "Look, don't pay any attention to them," she told him. She felt rather sorry for him. He certainly wasn't much of a dancer under the best of circumstances and being openly laughed at by

Fred and Ginger over there seemed to have thoroughly unnerved him. "You're doing fine," she added encouragingly.

"No, I'm not. I'm afraid I have two left feet." He cleared his throat. "I don't dance much, as you can probably tell."

"You need to relax, you're very stiff. And . . . uh, you really don't have to keep drawing a box with your feet. Although your boxes are extremely precise," she added tactfully.

The music ended. "Thank you for the dance," Linc said. "You've been very patient."

Jay and Melinda Sue sidled up to them. "Vanessa, love," Jay said with a snigger, "when you two dance at your *wedding*, I suggest you wear more protective footgear. Something along the line of a combat boot."

Melinda Sue dissolved into a fit of giggles. Linc's face reddened, but he said nothing. Vanessa could tell he was embarrassed. She wondered why she was empathizing with a fortune hunter, and decided that perhaps he wasn't one, after all. He certainly didn't act like any fortune hunter she'd ever met.

He'd wanted to meet her, he'd asked about her, he'd danced with her, although he definitely didn't seem to like dancing much. And the way he stared at her, as if he simply couldn't take his eyes off her . . . Vanessa put all the clues together. She recognized admiration when she ran across it.

She stared from him to Jay and Melinda Sue. Lincoln Scott didn't deserve to be ridiculed simply because he'd asked her to dance. Her temper, volatile and fierce, blazed to life on his behalf. "If you two don't stop laughing like a pair of crazed hyenas, I'm going to make you both sorry you were ever born."

Jay and Melinda Sue abruptly stopped laughing. Vanessa continued to glower at them as they backed away, mumbling apologies.

"I'm impressed!" Linc exclaimed. "You actually scared them!"

Vanessa smiled modestly. "I suppose I did."

"But how? Your threat was rather vague."

"True." She shrugged. "But the Ramsey temper is nothing to be taken lightly. I'm sure Jay and Melinda Sue think I'm capable of anything. I do seem to have acquired a . . . certain reputation." She flexed her fingers and smiled wickedly. There were times when she felt trapped in that reputation and wondered how to get out of it. And then there were times like this, when she relished using it to her advantage. "As Lexie Madison was so eager to tell you all about me, I presume she didn't tell you what *she* is."

"I think I figured out what she is from our brief conversation tonight." Linc flashed her a grin.

It had the oddest effect upon Vanessa. Her stomach seemed to somersault. They laughed together. He really was a marvelous-looking man, Vanessa thought, feeling suddenly strangely breathless.

"May I get you a drink?" Linc offered politely.

He looked so hopeful. Oh well, why not? Vanessa decided impulsively. She was feeling rather giddy and free. The result of vanquishing Jay and Melinda Sue, perhaps?

"I'll have a shot of rye on the rocks," she told him with a bit of a swagger.

"Rye on the rocks?" he repeated dubiously. "Are you sure?"

"Did you expect me to order some sweet, fruity drink with a little paper umbrella in it?" she asked mockingly. Actually, she did order that type of drink more often than not, but she had a certain image to maintain with Lincoln Scott. He believed her to be tough and fierce—and she had confirmed that image by rescuing him from Melinda Sue and Jay's sneers and snickers. A frozen peach daiquiri complete with tiny purple parasol simply would not suit in this instance.

"I didn't expect you to order something that tastes like liquid sandpaper," he said. "Are you sure that—"

"Of course I'm sure. In fact, make it a double." She admitted to herself that she was showing off a bit.

Looking doubtful, he went off to fulfill her demand. He returned a few minutes later with her double rye, along with a bourbon on the rocks for himself. She took the glass from him and lightly clinked it against his own. "Down the hatch," she said cheerfully, and took a healthy swallow.

And nearly spit it out. If there were such a thing as liquid sandpaper, it would undoubtedly taste like this, Vanessa thought, fighting the urge to shudder. She was very aware of Lincoln's Scott's eyes upon her.

"Perhaps you'd prefer something else?" he asked deferentially, but she was positive that she saw a certain gleam in his eye—the kind of teasing, challenging gleam that one of her brothers would get after daring her to do something that they thought she would never be able to do. Inevitably, invariably, Vanessa leaped to the challenge and forced herself to follow through, no matter how difficult or repulsive the deed.

She remembered eating a beetle because her brother Jed had suggested that girls were too sissy to do so. She remembered shivering with fright as she stood on a twenty-foot diving platform, staring at the lake below. Her brother Rad had taunted that girls were afraid of heights, and she'd immediately climbed up that ladder to jump off and prove him wrong. There were hundreds of other examples. From the time she'd been a small girl, she'd been determined to prove that a Ramsey female was just as brave, hardy—and, yes, reckless—as any Ramsey male.

Compared to some of the feats she'd endured, a double shot of rye was child's play. "No, this is just fine. Excellent rye," she said, and held her breath as she tossed the rest of the drink down her throat. It was easier that way. She didn't have to taste it as it burned a path from her tongue to her stomach.

Linc watched her, fascinated. She'd finished a double and he'd barely wet his tongue with his bourbon. Vanessa gave him a triumphant smile as she clutched her empty glass.

Her smile electrified him. Lord, she was beautiful. And daring, and exciting. He'd never met a woman like her. He stared at her, transfixed.

Vanessa was well aware of the effect her smile was having on him. She felt pleased and powerful. Most men she met were not as obvious about their feelings. They played it cool and spun all sorts of lines. She knew all about those games. There was something . . . refreshing in Lincoln Scott's open, unadulterated admiration.

And then she spied the flash of yellow and sheen of coppery red hair coming toward them. Yes, it was Lexie Madison and she was coming their way with a purposeful expression on her lovely face. Vanessa frowned.

"Hello again, Linc," Lexie greeted him with a charming smile, and Vanessa's frown deepened. "Isn't the band fantastic? I—"

"Yes, the band is quite good," Vanessa interrupted. "In fact, Lincoln and I were just going to have another dance." She slipped her hand through Linc's arm and noted his look of surprise, and Lexie's look of pure vexation. "Weren't we, Linc?" she added, smiling up at him for confirmation.

Of course, he was too much of a gentleman to deny it. "Yes, we were." He was such a gentleman that he appeared ready to apologize to Lexie for leaving her standing there. Vanessa didn't care for that idea at all. She tugged at his arm and he allowed her to pull him back out onto the dance floor.

It wasn't as if she feared competition from Lexie, Vanessa assured herself, casting a final glance at the smoldering redhead. That would imply jealousy, which would further imply that she felt possessive of Lincoln Scott. Which was not the case at all. She was merely doing Linc a favor by rescuing him from that game—playing vixen. He did not strike her as a man experienced with sexual games or vixens. Call it her good deed of the day.

"You're very brave to want to risk another dance," he said with a wry smile. "I happen to have a two-step variation of my box step. Maybe we'll have better luck with that."

Vanessa wasn't sure how to take his self-deprecatory humor. Ramseys did not self-deprecate. They didn't care to acknowledge shortcomings, even obvious ones. And when in doubt, they took charge, which she did now. "Stop worrying, Lincoln. I'm going to teach you how to dance."

They both noticed that he was still holding his drink. Vanessa glanced around, then called to a young man dancing with a pretty blonde a few feet away from them. Her voice managed to be both beguiling and authoritative. "Charlie, take Lincoln's glass and put it on a table somewhere," she instructed the young man who'd snapped to attention the moment she'd called his name. She handed him Linc's drink. "Thanks, Charlie. You're a sweetie."

Linc was amazed when Charlie took the glass and went off to do her bidding, leaving his partner standing alone in the middle of the dance floor.

"Sadly, my little girl has earned the reputation as something of a—well, I guess the modern term might be man-eater." Quentin Ramsey's voice suddenly echoed in Linc's head. *"But I have no doubt that you'll be able to cope with her, Lincoln, my boy. Your past record speaks well for you. You're as strong and determined and implacable as she is. Vanessa needs a man like you."*

Staring into Vanessa's shining gray eyes, Linc felt a tremor deep within him. Did she really need him? Could she ever want him? He knew he wanted her. If it was possible to fall in love with someone via photograph, he'd done it yesterday at his first sight of her.

And then Quentin Ramsey's voice sounded, unbidden, once more in his mind. *"Vanessa's tough,"* the older man had said with a touch of paternal pride. *"She's not going to passively fall into your arms. You'll have to win her, and doing so will probably require every ounce of that strength and determination and implacability of yours. But I have confidence in you, Linc. And to strengthen your resolve—and dissolve hers . . ."*

"First, don't hold me as if I were a broomstick." Vanessa's clear, compelling voice drowned out her father's and ended Linc's reverie. When Vanessa Ramsey wanted attention, she knew how to command it, Linc thought with an indulgent smile. And at this moment, she wanted his attention for the dancing lesson she was so graciously preparing to give him. She took his left hand in her right one and laid her other hand on his shoulder, then moved nearer to him, closing the gap between them.

Linc's hand folded around hers and he held it against his chest. Vanessa felt the warmth of his chest through the material of his white shirt. She drew in a shaky breath which turned into a soft gasp as Linc's other hand slid slowly, purposefully, from its proper place in the middle of her back down the length of her spine.

"Yes, this is much better," he said in a husky voice that seemed to have its own physical effect upon her. All at once, her knees were weak. She felt his hand spread wide across the small of her back, and when his fingers began to slowly, lightly caress her there, hot arrows of sensation pierced her innermost, secret places.

And then her heart seemed to stop, only to resume beating at a thundering gallop. For Linc was holding her so close to him that his physical response to her was unmistakable. He emanated white-hot, masculine heat.

Her eyes darted to his and were trapped by his deep sapphire gaze. They stared at each other for a long, silent moment. Vanessa felt something sharp and fiery leap within her as she gazed at his rugged, intense face. She felt her face grow warm as the blood raced frantically in her head. Her senses were spinning. The music seemed to be coming from some other dimension. For the first time in her memory, she missed a dance step and stumbled. Linc was there to steady her, to support her.

Reflexively, she leaned into him. Somehow, in the past few moments, everything had changed. She was no longer the one in charge. Suddenly, Lincoln Scott seemed very big and very strong and very male. He made her feel weak and vulnerable; his hold was no longer diffident, but possessive.

He'd dropped any pretense of dancing and was simply swaying to the music as he held her tight. In that slow and utterly determined way of his, he lightly nudged her thighs apart with his own muscular thigh.

Without thinking, Vanessa parted her legs and deepened the intimacy of their contact. She felt his arousal and shivered. Her breasts were flattened against his solid chest. She'd never been more aware of their rounded softness than at this moment, when they yielded to Linc's hard, masculine frame. She felt small and submissive, and the feelings, though tantalizing, were foreign to her. A mental alarm sounded in her head.

She jerked her head up and met his deep, dark blue eyes. "Lincoln, I—I don't want you to kiss me," she blurted out breathlessly.

Two

Linc held her gaze. "Don't you?" he asked softly.

Vanessa felt a surge of hot color in her cheeks. "No!" Though she would have rather died than admit it, she was aroused and nervous and thoroughly confused. What was happening to her? she wondered dizzily. It wasn't like her to melt and turn to mush in a man's arms. Far from it. She was used to calling all the shots in all situations, and that included her own responses and reactions.

"Let me go, Linc," she demanded, and was stunned by the husky thickness of her voice. She didn't sound at all like her usual, commanding self. When Vanessa Ramsey spoke, men jumped. They were afraid not to. But the voice she'd just heard wouldn't make anyone leap to do her bidding. It was soft and sexy and languorous. She couldn't blame Lincoln Scott for not heeding it.

She gulped. Held captive in Linc's arms, feeling his hard strength against her, inhaling the fresh soap-and-male scent of him, gazing into his oh-so-blue eyes, something was happening to her, all right. She was accustomed to being in cool command, but she wasn't cool or in command now. She felt on the verge of—of losing control. And not of her temper. That was a common enough occurrence in the life of Vanessa Ramsey. No, this liquid excitement bubbling through her was something else entirely.

For the first time ever, she was thinking with her hormones, Vanessa realized in amazement. And the results were unsettling and incredible to her. She knew she was usually slow to become sexually aroused; she'd long suspected that if there was romantic passion in her, it was buried under deep layers of guarded reserve.

The truth was, she didn't really like to be touched very much. But Lincoln Scott had delved effortlessly through those protective layers of hers. He was touching her and she was—she was liking it! And responding to it. His big hand was lightly kneading the sensitive spot at the small of her back. He was holding her close to him, but he wasn't groping or pawing or thrusting himself against her. Those were the usual masculine maneuverings employed to conquer her, and they inevitably roused only her contempt.

Linc wasn't moving at all. She was the one who was in motion, she realized in shock. She had arched herself against him and was slowly rotating her hips in rhythm to his gentle caresses.

Vanessa tried to still herself. She really tried, but she couldn't seem to do it. A liquid fire was racing through her veins, heating her, melting her. Her legs were beginning to tremble and her pulses throbbed heavily, in her throat, in her chest, between her legs . . .

"I feel so strange," she whispered, fighting the urge to close her eyes and lay her head against Linc's chest.

"Probably from that double shot of straight rye." His voice sounded above her head and she felt his warm breath rustle her hair. He sounded amused.

"No, I've never felt like this," she heard herself say. Her tongue seemed to be operating independently of her mind. "Liquor is not quicker with me, as a good number of would-be Romeos have learned the hard way."

"Exactly how do you feel, Vanessa?" Linc's voice

was quiet and calm. A nonjudgmental voice that encouraged one to confide.

How did she feel? Vanessa's fogged mind pondered that. "Amorous," she blurted out, and was aghast by the bluntness of her runaway tongue.

Linc's body shook strangely. With silent laughter, she realized in horror, and squeezed her eyes shut. "I won't tolerate being laughed at," she snapped. She was humiliated beyond belief.

"I'm not laughing at you, honey," he was quick to reassure her. Her head tilted back and she looked directly at him. He was smiling at her. There was both amusement and warmth in his blue eyes, something she'd never seen before in a man's eyes. Men found her exciting or threatening, often both, but never amusing. And the heat blazing in men's gazes when they looked at her was due to passion or frustration, often both, but not simple human warmth.

Vanessa trembled. She tightened her grip on him to steady herself.

"Why don't we go outside?" he suggested. "Some fresh air might clear your head."

"I'm not drunk, my head is perfectly clear," she insisted indignantly. "Believe me, if I were drunk you'd know it."

"You wouldn't be . . . er, amorous?"

She glared at him. "You *are* laughing at me, Lincoln Scott." She'd learned long ago that the best defense was a strong offense. It was time to turn the tables on him. "You deliberately tried to get me drunk," she accused. "And now you're trying to spirit me off to the terrace to—to seduce me!"

She waited for him to crumple with chagrin. He grinned at her instead. "I'm not the one who told you to down a double shot of straight rye in one gulp, Vanessa. If you'll recall, I tried to talk you out of ordering it in the first place."

"Yes, and it was all part of your fiendish plan. You knew if you objected I'd have no choice but to go through with it."

"I see." His lips twitched, but he managed to contain the laughter she saw sparkling in his eyes. "Well, then, I suppose I owe you an apology. And I certainly admire the way you saw through my fiendish plan."

This was not going the way Vanessa intended. It was time to drop this particular subject. "It's very warm in here," she told him haughtily. "I'm going outside on the terrace for some fresh air."

"Good idea," Linc said blandly. "Wish I'd thought of it." He hooked his arm around her waist as he walked her toward the wide double doors leading to the terrace.

Vanessa tried to keep up with his long-legged stride, but she was having difficulty. The heels of her shoes had suddenly become precariously high, and she tottered and stumbled in them. If Linc hadn't been holding her so firmly, she might very well have fallen.

"Damn shoes," she muttered, blaming them for her uncharacteristic clumsiness. Impulsively, she kicked them off.

"You've shrunk!" Linc exclaimed, grinning. "You're so little without your power shoes on."

She cast him a look of disapproval. "I'm nearly five-six and that's not little. It's quite tall." Her height was a sore point with her. She'd always wanted to be imposingly tall like her father and brothers. Even her mother was taller than she was. Vanessa viewed her failure to achieve an impressive height as just that—a failure. And failure affronted her. She didn't care to be reminded of it.

"You may carry my shoes," she said grandly, and pushed open the doors to step out onto the long, moonlit terrace.

Linc stared at the strappy sandals of hyacinth-colored leather, which he guessed were imported and cost a small fortune. Vanessa had discarded them as casually as she might toss away a tissue. With a resigned sigh, he picked up the shoes and tucked them under his arm.

Farther down the terrace, Vanessa had flopped onto a cushioned chaise longue and was staring up at the cloudy night sky. It was a mild night for April and a breeze rustled the leaves in the nearby trees.

Linc dropped into the wide, comfortable chair next to her and set her shoes on the ground. Vanessa did not acknowledge the shoes or his presence. He shifted in the chair. "Feels like rain," he said at last.

"Oh, Lord, spare me small talk about the weather!"

"You're right, it was a pathetic opening gambit. Let's talk about something infinitely more fascinating. You."

She cast him a swift, sharp look. Was he needling her? It was difficult to tell with him. He kept his expression so impassive, his voice so calm. And she wasn't thinking as clearly as she should be. She hadn't yet recovered her equilibrium from that sensual little scene with him out on the dance floor. Her head was still spinning, and it wasn't totally due to the rye. She had a sneaking suspicion that he'd gotten the best of her back there in the party room, and she strove to suppress that thoroughly intolerable notion. Vanessa Ramsey won every encounter, every time, she reminded herself.

"You know," he said casually, "you said if you were drunk I'd know it, but you never did get around to telling me how you'd act if you actually were . . . uh, three sheets to the wind. Not amorous, we've already resolved that point," he added, and his voice was so dry that she studied him with narrowed eyes.

Was he making fun of her? She wondered. Damn, she couldn't tell! If only her mind didn't feel as if it were wrapped in cotton gauze. No, she decided, he probably wasn't teasing her. He wouldn't dare, he wouldn't want to risk her outrage. No doubt he was simply trying to make conversation, and since she'd ruled the weather out as a topic, he was searching for another one.

"Do you get silly and giggle a lot?" he prompted. "Put a lampshade on your head and dance on tables?"

"Certainly not! I never *giggle!*" Vanessa shot him a scathing glance. His expression was blandly innocent, although she was definitely beginning to think he was baiting her. Well, she could certainly hold her own against the likes of Lincoln Scott. "I tend to be rather forceful," she told him. *A lampshade on my head, indeed!* "Impulsive and aggressive."

"Ah, a radical personality change from your usual demure, quiet self."

Vanessa scowled up at him. His tone was very droll. "And I don't really get *drunk*," she added, rather righteously. "Once in a great while, I may have had a little too much to drink, but I can count those times on the fingers of one hand."

"I see."

"I may appear free-spirited, but I'm actually a very controlled individual."

"Ah."

"You simply can't believe everything you hear about me."

"No?" He turned toward her and leaned forward in his chair.

"No!" For example, I did *not* try to drown Melinda Sue Harper in a bowl of punch. That's *her* side of it. I was just teaching her a lesson."

"This must have been the last time you had a little too much to drink," Linc surmised. "When you were acting forcefully, impulsively, and aggressively."

"Yes, it was. And I'm not sorry I dunked her head in the Johnsons' punch bowl, although it did make an awful mess. She had it coming. Mindy's a vicious gossip, and she was spreading nasty stories about a dear friend of mine who wasn't around to defend himself."

"Your loyalty is admirable. And I begin to see why Mindy and her fleet-footed dancing partner decided to vanish after you threatened them tonight," Linc said dryly.

Vanessa nodded, basking in the glow of his approval and undivided attention. Her gaze swept over him. He'd turned out to be quite different from what she'd originally thought he was. And then it occurred to her that, except for his name, she really knew nothing about the man at all. It was definitely time to rectify that.

"Now it's your turn to tell me about yourself," she said, treating him to the full force of the Ramsey smile. She sat up and swung her legs over the side of the chaise longue.

Her knees bumped Linc's. She hadn't realized that his chair was so close to the chaise, and that sitting on the edge of it would put her within touching distance of him.

Linc glanced down at the long, smooth expanse of her shapely thigh exposed by the high slit in the tight skirt of her silk dress. He swallowed hard and forced himself to breathe deeply. Her nearness was intoxicating. He inhaled her perfume, he gazed at her milky white skin. He remembered how soft she'd felt when he'd held her while they danced. It took every ounce of his legendary iron control to keep from reaching out and stroking the alluring bareness of her slender shoulders. What would she do if he followed his impulse and ran his hand over her lusciously exposed thigh? Merely the thought of doing so made him ache. He wanted her with a physical force that stunned him.

Vanessa was watching him, and didn't miss his intense masculine response to her. Her heart thudded heavily, and she suddenly felt breathless and very warm. She was long accustomed to men wanting her, and was alternately flattered, amused, or annoyed by the reactions she evoked in members of the opposite sex. But now she trembled a little. This was the first time that merely observing a man's aroused response to her had aroused her, too.

"Who are you, Lincoln Scott?" she asked huskily. "How do you know Jack and Coralie Wallace and why did they invite you to their party tonight? I've never seen you or heard of you before. Not even

Melinda Sue has, and she makes it a point to know everything about everyone."

Linc leaned closer and his leg rubbed against hers. An electrical current seemed to jolt through them simultaneously, and they both inhaled sharply.

Vanessa scooted back a little, too unnerved by her volatile response to him to consider her small retreat a loss in her perpetual game of one-upmanship. Linc stayed right where he was.

"I guess it's obvious that I don't belong with the country club set," he said with a shrug. "The other men at this party pay more for one tie than I paid for my entire suit. And it shows, of course."

Vanessa remembered the comment she'd made earlier to Melinda Sue about his clothes and suddenly felt quite small. She hadn't realized that he would be aware of such things.

But he was. His lips twisted into a crooked smile. "And when I drove my car to the door of the clubhouse, I thought the parking valet was going to faint. Believe me, in a sea of Mercedes, Ferraris, and Porsches, a ten-year-old Pacer stands out like a wart on the end of a witch's chin."

"You drive a ten-year-old Pacer?" Vanessa stared at him, goggle-eyed. "I've never known anyone who owned a Pacer, not even a brand-new one." She almost added that she'd never known anyone to keep a car for ten years, either, unless it was an antique classic. Which she knew the Pacer was not. But she decided that she must sound terribly snobbish and rude, so she tried to make amends. "Do you—uh—get excellent mileage out of it?"

Linc laughed good-naturedly. "Naturally. Numbers are very important to me. You see, I'm an actuary. I met Jack Wallace when he hired my firm to do some actuarial consulting for his company and—"

"You're an *actuary*?" Vanessa interrupted, astonished. "Don't they compile mortality tables for insurance companies?" She gave a delicate shudder. "A somewhat ghoulish line of work, I'd say."

"Most people do associate actuaries with insurance companies, but there's more to actuarial work than that. Last year I left the insurance company I worked for to set up my own firm here in Houston. So far there's just me and an assistant and a secretary-receptionist, but the potential for expansion is there. We've been quite successful."

"You have?" she asked rather doubtfully. If he was quite successful, why were his clothes from a discount close-out sale and why did he drive an old car?

Linc had no trouble following her line of reasoning. "You're wondering why I don't dress and drive like a Yuppie if I'm so successful?"

"Well, yes, I suppose I am."

"Most of my money has gone to my family. You see, they own a farm in Kansas and I've been helping to keep them from going under financially. I'm sure you've heard about the farm crisis and—"

"A farm in Kansas?" she interrupted once more. "Is there a dog named Toto, too?"

He smiled. "The dog's name is Spot."

She stared at him. "You're not making this up, are you? There really is a family farm in Kansas?"

He nodded. "It belongs to my foster family, the Harrisons. They took me in when I was orphaned at twelve and treated me like one of their own. My foster father died five years ago and I'd promised him that I'd do whatever I could to keep the family on the farm. It's their home and they love it. I'll never let the bank take it from them."

"Didn't I see a movie with this plot? The noble farm family fights the evil bankers to keep their land?"

"A cliché, I know." He laughed. "Let's just hope that my family's story has a happy ending like in all those movies."

She had to admire him for not taking umbrage, Vanessa thought warmly. She had sounded—well—perhaps a little cynical about his family's plight. But he was good-natured and confident enough not to let her tactlessness upset him.

She felt an urge to make up for her caustic tongue. And what better way than to ask about his work? She knew how much men adored talking about their work, however deadly dull others might find it. "What does an actuary do in an actuarial firm, Linc?" she asked with the charming and attentive politeness of a finishing school graduate.

Linc's face lit with enthusiasm, and his smile and glowing blue eyes took her breath away. "Well, I design and implement retirement funds—you know, set up pension plans for companies or individuals. And I'm frequently hired by divorce lawyers to value pension assets in order to attach a balance to a spouse's pension in the divorce settlement. I've also been called to testify in suits involving lost benefits due to job termination or accident and personal injury claims."

Vanessa nodded. "I guess that's the real glamour stuff, hmm? As opposed to compiling mortuary tables?"

"Mortality," Linc corrected her, and smiled. He was always happy to talk about his work and was delighted that Vanessa seemed interested in it. "It's really fascinating work," he said, and launched into an enthusiastic monologue on investigating and analyzing statistical data.

Vanessa's mind began to wander. She couldn't seen to stop staring at him. How could a man as good-looking and sexy—yes, he was sexy, exuding a virile energy that she simply couldn't deny— How could a man who looked like Lincoln Scott get so fired up over *numbers*? She vaguely recalled the math majors she'd known in college. Hadn't they all been short and skinny with thick glasses and nerd packs in their shirt pockets?

Men with Lincoln Scott's physical attributes were supposed to be smooth, fast-talking charmers who used their great looks and fantastic bodies to seduce women by the score. She ought to know, she'd been fending off that type for years. But this was the first time in her life that she'd been alone with an Adonis on a secluded terrace and been subjected to an incomprehensible discourse on—*actuarial work*?

She thought of her voluptuous response to him when they were dancing, of the tremor that had shaken her just moments ago when his leg had touched hers. And she felt a sudden, fierce regret. For she knew that in a minute or two, she was going to go back in to the party and never see Lincoln Scott again. Despite the inexplicable chemistry that sizzled between them, he was not for her. Not an actuary who drove a ten-year-old Pacer.

She knew that her reputation as a spoiled princess with a predilection for wild, extravagant behavior was highly exaggerated, but she was also aware that it had some basis in fact. She dated rich men who moved in fast circles, she lived the high life with glamour and excitement taken as a given. There was no way that a sedate, hard-working actuary dedicated to saving the family farm back in good old Kansas could fit into her lifestyle. She was enough of a realist to recognize that they inhabited two different worlds and enough of a pessimist to believe that sexual chemistry couldn't bridge them. It simply would never work.

She stared at him and a sudden surge of anger coursed through her. Knowing all that, why couldn't she forget the way his body had felt against hers while they danced? She tried to remind herself that he was an awful dancer. And that he was an actuary who was sitting out here in the moonlight with her, talking pensions and profit-sharing and something called 401-k plans.

But she still felt cheated. And confused and unhappy and it just wasn't fair. And somehow it was all his fault.

"I just remembered something else about actuaries," she cut in. She was used to being fawned over, not statistically deluged, she reminded herself. "Everybody makes jokes about how incredibly dull they are. Aren't actuaries supposed to make FBI agents look flashy and CPA's look zany?" She felt obliged to clarify it further, in case he missed the humor. "You see, FBI agents dress very conservatively and CPA's are the antithesis of zany."

"I get your point," Linc replied dryly.

"And to think that when I first saw you I thought you were a fortune hunter!" She laughed in spite of herself. "What self-respecting fortune hunter would become an *actuary*, of all things?" She laughed again at the very thought.

"I'm glad my profession provides you with so much amusement," Linc drawled.

She postponed her leaving long enough to ask, "So, why did you want to meet me? Do you want to compile some mortality statistics on me? Well, I don't smoke, I use seatbelts, and I'm a very light social drinker. There are no serious inherited illnesses running through our family. Or perhaps you'd rather discuss a pension plan? After all, I turned twenty-five last week and one can't start too early on these things, hmm?"

"I felt we should meet because your father wants me to marry you," Linc said in the same calm, flat tone he had used when he'd said it felt like rain.

Vanessa's smile froze. For a full moment, she sat stock still and stared at him. He wasn't smiling, his blue eyes held no teasing twinkle. Actuaries didn't make jokes, did they? *But he couldn't be serious!*

"I was as incredulous as you," Linc said, when it was obvious that Vanessa was bereft of speech. "I'd never even met your father, although I'd heard of him, of course. Who in Houston hadn't? But it seems that he'd heard of me from the actuarial consulting work I'd done for some of his business colleagues. Yesterday he called and asked me to come to his office. I thought he wanted my services in actuarial consulting. It turned out that he wanted me for a son-in-law."

"I think you're insane!" Vanessa found her voice again. "My father might have a well-known penchant for wanting his children to marry, but this is ridiculous!"

"At first I thought so, too. And I couldn't help but wonder why the daughter of a zillionaire needed her father to find a husband for her. I thought you must weigh three hundred fifty pounds and have a face that even the world's most expensive plastic surgeons couldn't fix. But your father was quick to show me your pictures and dispel that notion. You're very beautiful, Vanessa, but of course you know that."

"I'm not going to thank you for that actuarial version of a compliment!"

"It wasn't a compliment, it was a statement of fact," Linc continued dispassionately. "You look like a model for one of those high-fashion magazine covers. So I had to come up with another reason why your father might need to find you a husband. I thought perhaps you were singularly stupid—so bird-brained that not even your family's money was adequate compensation for a prospective bridegroom."

"Oh!" Vanessa was incensed. She abruptly stood up. "For your information, Mr. Scott, I am *not* stupid!" She couldn't remember the last time she'd been this enraged. Perhaps the time she'd pushed Melinda Sue's face into the champagne punch. She was rather sorry that there wasn't a similar weapon handy now.

Linc rose to his feet. "No, I can see that you're not. And I'm glad. I don't think I could be very happy with a stupid wife."

His action brought him within inches of her. Vanessa jumped back and came perilously close to falling backward over the chaise. She probably would have if Linc hadn't reached out to grab her.

"I'm *not* going to be your wife!" she snapped. His hands were warm and heavy on her bare shoulders.

Her heart was hammering in her chest—from pure rage, she insisted to herself. She tried to wriggle away from him. "Take your hands off me! I don't want you to touch me!"

"We're not going to have much of a marriage if I can't touch you," Linc pointed out ingenuously.

Her eyes involuntarily dropped to his hands, his big hands with the long, well-shaped fingers and clean, square-cut nails. The sudden image of him touching her within the intimacy of marriage flashed before her mind's eye. A frisson of heat rippled through her, unnerving her. "We're not going to have any marriage!" she cried. "I'm not going to marry you!"

Linc nodded his head. He was calm, implacable. He knew now what the astute Quentin Ramsey had been the first to divine. He was going to be her husband, she was the woman for him. "Yes, you will, Vanessa."

"No!"

"Yes."

If he was the epitome of the immovable object, then she was the irresistible force. Their eyes clashed as their wills collided. The resounding crash was silent, but shook them both.

Three

The silence was profound, tension-charged. Vibrations of sexual energy hummed between them. Linc felt his renowned common sense and practicality rapidly dissolve along with his usually unassailable willpower.

Once his hands were on her, the urge to pull her those few extra inches into his arms proved to be too irresistible a temptation for him to overcome. So he gave in to it. His hands swept possessively down her back and he molded her against him.

Vanessa saw the blue fire burning in his eyes. She felt the muscular columns of his thighs hard against her and fought the sudden tremulousness that crept into her limbs. She clenched her hands into fists and pushed against his chest to break free. And didn't succeed. He held her closer and buried his lips in the soft, scented hollow of her throat. He nibbled sensuously along the slender, sensitive curve of her neck and she whimpered with pleasure. Slowly, her fists uncurled and her hands slipped to his shoulders. She clung to him, feeling his muscles ripple beneath her palms as she caressed him.

"Vanessa." The passion in his voice when he spoke her name sent a rush of desire through her. The male sound and smell and shape of him surrounded her. She felt her breasts tighten as liquid fire burned a path from her belly to the dark, secret place below.

Her bones seemed to be turning to marshmallow as her body leaned into his, melting against his unyielding masculine frame.

She watched his head lower to hers and stared, transfixed by the fine, sensual lines of his mouth. She tried to breathe, but there didn't seem to be any air in her lungs. Vaguely, she recalled that she was furious with him and that she ought to be fighting for her freedom. But that seemed to be memories of another Vanessa in another lifetime. All she wanted now was to feel his mouth on hers. She wanted to taste him. She shuddered with need and murmured his name.

"Do you want me as much as I want you, Vanessa?" Linc asked, his lips poised tantalizingly above hers. No woman had ever had this wild, explosive effect upon him. When he took Vanessa in his arms, the careful, controlled actuary that he knew himself to be was transformed into a passionate, sensual man that he'd never dreamed he would become. It was exciting and exhilarating. His hands roamed over her possessively, arousingly. He knew she was as hungry for him as he was for her, but he wanted to hear her say it. Hell, he *needed* to hear her say it. He had to make her aware of and admit her need for him.

He nipped teasingly at her lips and she protested the sensual torment with a small moan. "Say it, Vanessa!"

Vanessa quivered. He sounded sexy and commanding and very male, and she forgot that she was Vanessa Ramsey, whom no man dared to command. She forgot that he was an actuary with a ten-year-old Pacer and a family farm to save and was therefore totally unsuitable for her. She even forgot his crazy claim about her father wanting him to marry her. "Yes, Linc," she breathed in a sexy, submissive, and very feminine voice that she scarcely recognized as her own. "I want you."

And then his mouth was on hers and she felt

fireworks explode in her head. His lips brushed lightly over hers, moving softly back and forth until a breathless little moan escaped from her throat. His tongue slipped between her parted lips to probe the hot, moist hollow of her mouth.

Her fingers tangled in his thick blond hair and she pressed herself tightly against him. His tongue rubbed and stroked hers in an erotic rhythm that made her throb and burn with a sweet, sensual fire. Clinging to him, she trembled in urgent response to their ardor.

His hand covered her breast in a gesture of pure possession and he murmured something dark and sexy into her mouth. Vanessa moved provocatively against his hand as a spiral of exquisite pleasure spun through her. His thumb glided gently, purposefully over her nipple as it tightened and hardened under his caress.

The kiss went on and on, becoming deeper, hotter, even more intimate. Standing became too difficult and by unspoken mutual consent, they sank down onto the cushions of the chaise longue. Vanessa wrapped her arms around Linc, as she moved sensuously against him. She loved the feel of his warm weight upon her. It felt so good, so right to lie beneath him this way.

He nuzzled her ears and her neck and trailed kisses along the delicate curve of her jaw. Finally, she captured his chin between her hands and guided his mouth to hers.

Still, Linc didn't kiss her with the hot, hard pressure she craved. He lightly touched his lips to hers in a maddening and totally unsatisfying series of quick, staccato kisses.

"Linc," she protested breathlessly. "Kiss me hard."

He gazed at her, his eyes glittering with hunger. "That's the way I like it, too," he rasped. "Hot and hard and deep."

His mouth opened over hers, and her eyelids fluttered shut as she welcomed his tongue into the moist warmth of her mouth. She arched her body against his, wanting him to touch her, aching for it. When his big, warm hand slipped beneath the cool silk to cup the rounded softness of her small breast, she sighed with satisfaction.

The large, cold drop of water hit Vanessa's arm at the same time that another fat droplet landed on Linc's neck. Both were too caught up in the whirl of passion to make any sense of it. They ignored the next few drops which splattered on them, too. But the deluge that suddenly burst forth from the sky in the next few moments could not be ignored.

It was as if the heavens had opened up to let loose an ocean of water upon the earth. The rain was cold, driving, and heavy, and a sudden wind swept torrents of it in sheets along the long length of the terrace.

Linc and Vanessa sprang to their feet in total shock. They were thoroughly drenched within seconds. "Come on!" yelled Linc as a loud clap of thunder echoed in the sky. He caught her hand and began to run toward the doors, half dragging Vanessa along behind him.

"This is terrible!" she spluttered, half blinded by the driving rain beating upon her face. "I'm all wet! I'm cold! I—I hate this!" A jagged bolt of lightning lit up the sky and she shrieked. She had been thrust from the exciting, warm cocoon of passion into a cold spring thunderstorm and the transformation had been too shocking, too abrupt. The emotions and sensations pouring through her were wild and intense, and the realization of just how completely she had surrendered to Lincoln Scott sent her reeling. She felt exposed and vulnerable. And cold and wet. And suddenly, intensely furious.

Linc ran past the doors to the party room to another set of doors farther up the terrace. The room was dark and he realized his mistake and hauled her back to the correct set of doors. Which were locked. He cursed and rattled the brass door knobs, to no avail.

"You let me inside this minute, Lincoln Scott!" Vanessa demanded, pushing a handful of her thick, soaked hair away from her face. What felt like gallons of water came splashing down on her head, and she howled. "This is all your fault!"

"Vanessa, the doors must've automatically locked shut after we went out. I didn't do it."

His calm, rational explanation served only to ignite her temper to the flash point. "You knew this was going to happen. You did this on purpose."

"Sorry, honey, I can't take responsibility for making it rain." And then he compounded his error by laughing.

"It's not funny! You lured me outside and—"

"Lured you? Vanessa, if you'll remember, I *followed* you out."

She ignored that. "You knew it was going to rain. 'Feels like rain,' you said with a—a diabolical gleam in your eye. You had this all planned, you—you actuary!"

Linc cast her an exasperated glance. There was another jarring rumble of thunder and a bright flash of lightning streaked the sky. Vanessa rather dramatically shut her eyes and covered her ears with her hands. Linc began to pound on the locked doors. "Open the doors!" he called over and over again.

"You're making an awful scene!" scolded Vanessa.

"Honey, anybody who dunks someone in a punch bowl at a party can hardly complain about being involved in a scene." He continued to pound at the doors. The rain continued to pound down on them.

The doors were opened a few minutes later by a lovely, lithe redhead in a yellow dress of crepe de chine. Vanessa groaned. What else could she have expected? she railed crossly to herself. Naturally, Lexie Madison would be the one to hear Linc pounding and come to open the doors. It was simply that kind of a night.

"Vanessa!" Lexie exclaimed, jumping aside as Vanessa pushed inside. "You look like a drowned rat! I've never seen your hair such a mess, not even after swimming! And your eye makeup is all over your face!"

She sounded positively joyful and Vanessa glowered at her. Then Linc stepped inside and Lexie's smile faded. "Were you two out there together?" she asked, her eyes darting from Vanessa to Linc.

"Yes. He proposed to me and I turned him down," Vanessa snapped.

Lexie laughed. "Oh, Vanessa, you say the most outrageous things." She turned to Linc. "Gracious, Linc, you poor thing, you're all wet! Let me—"

"My shoes!" Vanessa interrupted with a wail. "They're still out there!" She caught Linc's arm and tried to pull him to the door. "Go get them, Linc."

"Why should he get your shoes?" Lexie glared daggers at her. "Get them yourself!"

"You have to get them, Lincoln," Vanessa insisted. "You're the one who carried them out, remember?"

"At your request, madam," Linc reminded her. "Or was it at your command?"

"I don't care, just go get my shoes." A gust of wind blew a fierce blast of rain in from the terrace and she shivered. "I don't want to go back out in that!"

"What makes you think I do?" Linc asked.

"It's only rain, Lincoln, you're not sugar, you won't melt! Anyway, you have to. If my shoes are out there any longer, they're going to be ruined."

"Linc, don't pay any attention to her," Lexie inserted coolly. "The Ramseys tend to think that the rest of us exist merely to serve them. Vanessa in particular harbors that delusion."

"I do not!" Vanessa protested hotly. "All right, I'll get my shoes myself. I'll go out into the wind and rain, even though I'm already soaked to the skin and freezing cold." She paused dramatically on the threshold. "I could be struck by lightning, you know."

"We should be so lucky!" Lexie said with an acid smile.

Vanessa cast Lincoln an imploring glance. Her gray eyes were huge and sad, her beautiful mouth quivered. "Please, Lincoln," she said softly.

Linc was fully aware that he was being manipulated by an expert in the field. She'd probably learned at the age of two that flashing those big eyes and arranging her adorable mouth just so dissolved whatever opposition stood in her way. She was so spoiled, he mused. Hilariously spoiled.

He heard her father's voice echo once more in his head. *Vanessa is a butterfly and you're the only man I can visualize as the net necessary to restrain her. Not hurt her, not break her, but keep her safe.*

Linc gave his head a shake as he thought of yesterday's bizarre interview with Quentin Ramsey. It had been somewhat disorienting to hear himself referred to as a butterfly net. In fact, the entire episode had been disquieting in the extreme, he reflected. What kind of man chose his daughter's husband and then attempted to seal the deal with an offer that approached the realm of fantasy? A hard-headed, unsentimental man, obviously. A man of unlimited power and money and the bold insensitivity to use both to achieve his aims. That described Quentin Ramsey perfectly.

Linc doubted that Vanessa had ever come up against her father's resolute, unyielding side. She'd been petted and adored her entire life and radiated the confidence which resulted from such an upbringing. Would she be crushed when she realized that her doting father had taken it upon himself to seal her fate? Linc knew he didn't want that to happen. He liked her high spirits and breezy air of self-confidence. He wanted to protect her, to continue the petting and adoring. But on a different level. He wanted her as a woman, not as a spoiled little girl.

Still, she was irresistible as she stood in the door

gazing at him like a forlorn kitten about to be cast out into the cold cruel world. "Get away from the door, Vanessa." He sighed, bowing to the inevitable. "I'll get your shoes."

Vanessa's face lit up. "Oh, thank you, Linc!" she murmured.

He felt as if he'd been dealt a blow directly to his solar plexus. Even soaking wet, with her eye makeup running in rivulets down her cheeks and her hair drenched and hanging in rattails around her face, she dazzled him.

Vanessa and Lexie watched him dash out into the storm, which gave no signs of relenting. "The most gorgeous-looking guy to come along in ages and *you* already have your claws in him!" Lexie groused, tossing a glare at Vanessa. "I suppose it doesn't matter to you that I saw him first. That he was with me at this party until you decided to move in on us."

"I didn't move in on you," protested Vanessa. "He—" She broke off, frowning. Why bother to defend herself? Lexie would continue to believe what she wanted to believe anyway. Perhaps she should mention that Linc was an actuary who drove a ten-year-old Pacer. And then she could casually add that nearly all his money was earmarked for the family farm in Kansas. It might be fun to watch Lexie turn green or purple or whatever color disappointed gold-digging redheads turn.

Her thoughts jumped to Lincoln Scott's bald pronouncement about her father wanting him to marry her. Could it be some new kind of fortune-hunting approach? she mused, and the chill that coursed through her had nothing to do with her wet clothing.

Images of herself lying in Linc's arms outside on the chaise flashed in her mind, and a surge of heat replaced her inner chill. He'd managed to touch her—both literally and figuratively—in a way that no other man ever had. She quivered. It was definitely time to distance herself—both literally and figuratively—from him.

Linc returned with her shoes a moment later. "Milady's slippers," he said, handing them to her with a flourish.

Vanessa took the sodden scraps of leather from him and dangled them by the straps, frowning her distaste. "I don't want to put them on, they're too wet. It's definitely time for me to go home. Lexie, make my good-byes to Coralie and Jack."

"Okay, okay," grumbled Lexie. She watched Vanessa stride off, carrying her shoes, then turned quickly to Linc. "Linc, you don't have to leave. We'll get you some towels from the men's locker room and—"

He didn't bother to turn around. He was already following Vanessa out of the room and down the hall. "I'll drive you home," he announced when he caught up with her.

"Not in a million years," Vanessa replied coolly as she made her way along the lushly carpeted hallway.

"I can't let you drive. Not after that rye you drank. And certainly not in this storm."

"I'm completely capable of driving myself, thank you. And I make it a point never to go off with strangers."

"I'm hardly a stranger, Vanessa. Not after what happened between us tonight."

"Nothing happened between us!" she snapped, though her face flushed scarlet. Oh, Lord, she was blushing. Like some gauche and flustered adolescent! Vanessa was aghast.

"Vanessa, if it hadn't started to rain, we—"

"But it did start to rain, didn't it?" she interrupted, whirling round to face him. "And I came to my senses just in time. So get yourself lost, Mr. Lincoln Scott. I don't want you hanging around me, I don't want to hear any more of your stupid lies."

"I haven't lied to you, Vanessa. And I never intend to." He stared down at her for a long moment. And then, "Did you ever read *The Godfather*, Vanessa?"

"What?" She was thoroughly flummoxed by his seeming non sequitur. And she hated being flummoxed. Once again he'd succeeded in throwing her off balance.

"If you didn't read the book, perhaps you saw the movie?" Linc persisted with a dogged patience that set her teeth on edge.

"Are you insinuating that I don't read? I'm not stupid, we've already covered that. And I do read—constantly—everything I can get my hands on! And yes, dammit, I did read *The Godfather*, for whatever that has to do with anything!"

"Don't swear," Linc admonished lightly. "I realize you have your rough, tough reputation to maintain, but I don't like to hear women curse." His lips twitched. "Particularly not my fiancée."

"If you dare to mention the word fiancée or marriage one more time, I'll—I'll—" She gazed wildly around the hallway, as she pondered what was heinous enough to threaten him with.

"I mentioned *The Godfather* in reference to that one passage, where the Don makes the Hollywood producer an offer he couldn't refuse," Linc continued, as if she hadn't spoken. "Do you remember that part, Vanessa?"

She stood motionless under his piercing blue gaze and saw the intensity burning in his eyes. She took a step backward. "Yes, I remember." To her consternation, her voice was not as forceful or as sharp as she would have liked.

"That scene was reenacted yesterday afternoon between your father and me in his office, Vanessa. He made me an offer I literally can't refuse."

He was so serious, so methodically insistent. She knew he wasn't joking and she'd already ruled out mental derangement. That meant . . . Her stomach heaved. "You're saying that my father made you some kind of offer"—she gulped—"to marry me?"

Lincoln Scott nodded solemnly.

She pondered the notion for a full ten seconds before furiously rejecting it. He wasn't joking or crazy, so that made him a liar. "And you expect me to believe that? I'm supposed to believe that my father bribed an actuary—one I'd never even met—to marry me?"

"It's true we hadn't met then, but that was a simple problem, easily remedied. Your father called Jack Wallace and asked him to invite me to this party tonight."

"And now we've met." Vanessa's eyes widened in horror. And they had struck sparks like a match to a powderkeg. She quivered at the memory. This couldn't have been planned, she couldn't have been set up by her father and this actuary! "N-No! I still don't believe you!"

"Your father suggested that I sweep you off your feet. Somehow, I was supposed to make you fall madly in love with me tonight."

Vanessa glowered at him. She pictured herself melting in his arms, sensuously whimpering for his kisses, and she went rigid. "Not a chance, mister."

"That's what I thought, too," Linc agreed amiably. "I'm not one for intrigue or deception—and I knew I could never credibly romance a woman like you. I thought it best to be straightforward and honest and tell you the whos, whats, and wherefores of your father's plan."

"My father doesn't have a plan to marry me off to you! And if he did . . . Oh, if he did . . ." Her voice trailed off and her temper smoldered. Hot flames of fury burned in her. "Well, he just wouldn't dare to try such a thing! It would never work! As if I'd ever marry anyone because my father engineered it!"

"The way things stand, you don't have much choice in the matter," Linc said in that maddeningly calm voice of his. "Your father and I have already agreed that you and I will be married."

Well, not quite, he silently amended, but she didn't have to know that. He had only agreed to meet Vanessa at this party tonight, his curiosity and interest—and yes, his passion—having been fired by those eye-popping pictures of her. What normal, red-blooded American male could resist the chance of meeting such a beauty? Linc had asked himself in Quentin's office yesterday afternoon. And he'd promised himself that if she turned out to be unbearable or insufferable he would take off with no one the wiser.

"You and Daddy have decided?" Vanessa repeated archly. "What about me? Don't I have a say in the matter? This is twentieth-century Houston, Texas, we're living in, not medieval Europe. In case you haven't heard, the bride has a hand in selecting her groom these days."

Linc smiled. "Your father is expecting you to select me."

Once again his smile unsettled her. He was so relentlessly serious most of the time that one of his smiles seemed like a special treat. Vanessa was instantly disgusted with herself for even daring to think such an insipid thing. Her wrath intensified. "After you supposedly swept me off my feet—as if *I* would ever fall for *you*—"

"I worried about that myself, at first," Linc interrupted softly. "But I'm not worried anymore. You're sexually attracted to me, Vanessa, though you're determined to deny it . . . now. But you showed me all I needed to know out on the terrace."

"No!" Her voice rose shrilly. She wasn't sexually attracted to this man, she hadn't fallen for him! she silently wailed. His clothes were wrong, his profession was wrong, his car was *terribly* wrong. She had a checklist of requirements for her Mr. Right and Lincoln Scott had failed in three of the top categories. "I refuse to listen to another word! You're deliberately trying to—to—"

"I'm simply pointing out what you're trying very hard to deny, Vanessa. That you want me as much as I want you. You admitted it out on the terrace. Why won't you let yourself admit it now?"

And then he reached for her and took her in his arms and she immediately felt the way she had the last time he'd held her. Soft and feminine and pliant. Breathless with a kind of wanting that she'd never experienced before. If he kissed her again . . .

"It's going to be good between us, Vanessa," Linc said in a soft, soothing voice that made her want to snuggle closer and lose herself in the comfort of his arms. "I'll try my best to make you happy." His hands moved over her back, pressing her closer with warm, open-palmed caresses. "And I've always managed to succeed in whatever I set out to do."

"This is crazy," Vanessa said. Her head was spinning again.

"I know." Linc's hand drifted lower to cup the sweetly rounded softness of her bottom. One long finger traced the enticing cleft through the wet silk of her dress.

Vanessa felt a jolt of electricity shoot along the length of her spine. And she panicked at the wild response he so effortlessly evoked in her. He made her feel, made her want . . . His power over her was alarming. He could even make her say things . . . Her thoughts tumbled incoherently through her brain. "Let me go!" she demanded hoarsely. "I want to go home."

"I'm going to take you home, honey." His lips brushed her forehead.

She jerked away from him in a defensive fury. "No, you aren't. I'm not going anywhere with you. I hate you!"

"No, you don't, Vanessa." Linc sighed. "Your father warned me it was probably going to be one helluva courtship."

"We aren't going to have a courtship—or a marriage! How many times do I have to say it? How many ways do I have to say it?" She searched frantically for the words to convince him. Fury hadn't done it, perhaps she would play it his way. Rational and calm. "Look, its nothing personal, Lincoln, but you—you just aren't my type!"

It was an almost laughable pronouncement in view

of her incendiary response to him and she knew it and thought she would die if he called her on it. Or if he laughed at her. She felt vulnerable and uncertain, and she hated the feeling.

"Your father fully agrees that I'm not the type of man you seem to prefer," Linc said quietly. "That's one reason why he chose me to be your husband. He detests your taste in men. Said you've dated the sorriest collection of wimps and jerks that he'd ever seen."

How did one get the better of a man who refused to take offense? Vanessa wondered wildly. He was so—so reasonable. So logical. It was maddening. "You're hopelessly intractable!" she accused.

"And implacable and determined," he agreed easily. "Qualities your father assured me were essential when it came to dealing with you."

She resisted the urge to scream and gritted out words instead. "That's it! I'm not wasting another moment trying to—" Her voice ground to a halt. He had her so off balance that she wasn't even sure what she was trying to say to him. There were times when the only sound strategy was to beat a hasty retreat, and though it killed her to admit it, this was one of those times. Lincoln Scott had won this encounter and he knew it. She knew it, too, and the knowledge enraged her. She stalked off, her head held high in the air.

Linc followed her, his mouth curved into a reluctant smile. Even dripping wet, she pulled off the queen-in-high-dudgeon act with aplomb.

She strode outside to stand under the overhang of the front steps of the club's posh colonial façade. It was still raining hard with no signs of the storm abating. Two parking attendants jumped to attention, obviously astonished by her shoeless, drenched condition. "I'll get your car for you, Miss Ramsey," a short, slim teen-age boy volunteered eagerly.

"Thank you, Jody." She gave him a warm smile.

Linc stepped beside her. "Vanessa, I'll drive you home in your car if you prefer, but—"

Vanessa's smile disappeared. "Jody, this man is harassing me. Will you please alert security at the gate and ask them to come to my assistance?"

"Yes, Miss Ramsey," Jody said importantly, then turned to the other attendant, an even shorter, skinnier teenager. "Tommy, you stay right here with Miss Ramsey and don't let that man har—hur—bother her, you hear?"

Jody dashed out into the storm. Tommy trotted to Vanessa's side like an obedient puppy and scowled at Linc in disapproval. "You don't bother Miss Ramsey, mister," he ordered.

Linc sighed with exasperation. "I'm not bothering Miss Ramsey. And I need my car."

The boy regarded him with stony silence. Vanessa took a step closer to her protector, who barely reached her shoulder, and rewarded him with a dazzling smile of approval. Linc sighed again, and the three of them stood silently, watching the rain pound the pavement of the wide, circular drive.

The loyal Jody arrived in Vanessa's champagne-colored Ferrari Testarossa with two Houston police officers, moonlighting as security guards for the club, following in an unmarked car. They were only too glad to detain Linc with a battery of questions while Vanessa handed generous tips to Tommy and Jody and then slipped behind the wheel of her car.

She rolled down her window and rain water splashed onto her face. "Officers, you can let him go now," she called. "And get his car for him, boys. I don't think I have to worry about him chasing and catching up to me in his ten-year-old Pacer."

The four glanced from Linc to Vanessa in her sleek two-door coupe and burst into hearty peals of laughter at the image of an old Pacer pursuing the splendid new racing car. Vanessa joined briefly in the laughter, then called good night and raced out into the rain, tires screeching.

"Some car!" Jody rhapsodized. "The Ramseys always drive the sharpest, coolest cars."

"Some woman," said one of the guards admiringly, and the others murmured their assent. "She's like her car. Sharp and cool."

"And sexy," put in young Tommy.

There was ribald masculine agreement on that from everyone but Linc, who stood in silence, his hands shoved deep into his pockets as he watched the taillights of Vanessa's car fade from sight.

Four

The heavy rain made visibility poor and Vanessa slowed considerably after her expeditious departure from the club. She was carefully negotiating the highway exit ramp at all of ten miles per hour when she saw the headlights coming toward her. She narrowed her brows in split-second confusion. Headlights? Impossible. This was the exit ramp, with one-way traffic only.

Unless . . . Her eyes widened in horrified comprehension. Unless a driver ignored the WRONG WAY: DO NOT ENTER signs and tried to get to the highway via the exit ramp. The big car with the blinding headlights which was speeding toward her had obviously done just that.

Vanessa felt cold fingers of panic squeeze her throat and she froze. She had no retreat, there was a truck several yards behind her on the ramp. She heard a jarring blast of a car horn and realized in astonishment that the driver of the car coming toward her was blaring his horn *at her*!

Her immobilizing panic was momentarily replaced by indignation, enabling her to act. She swerved the car to one side to avoid a head-on collision and hit the guard rail. Still, those seconds had allowed her to achieve her goal. The other car missed smashing into the front of her car, sideswiping it instead as it bounced off the metal guard rail.

Unfortunately, the impact caused her car to skid on the rainslick road. It spun giddily and then crashed through the guard rail. Vanessa's hands clutched the steering wheel, although she realized that the car was out of control. Engulfed by a numbing calm, she felt the Ferrari Testarossa flip as it went over the six-foot grassy embankment.

This was it, then. The flat, fatalistic thought drifted through the shock-induced fog which shrouded her mind. There were so many things that she was never going to have a chance to experience. Meaningful work, a deep and abiding love, a child of her own . . . She was grateful for the peculiar numbness which seemed to have distanced her from the reality of her loss. All she could feel was a kind of detached regret.

Oddly, a very clear vision of Lincoln Scott came to her. She was mildly astonished that her last thoughts on this earth were to be of him, a stranger whom she'd just met. And then she didn't think at all, for the car came to an abrupt and stunning halt.

Vanessa didn't move, she was almost afraid to. Time seemed to have come to a halt as well, for the car's clock showed that less than a minute had elapsed since the initial collision with the guard rail. She finally dared to glance slowly around her. Her car had landed in an upright position. The windshield was shattered, but the glass remained intact. She became aware that the horn was blaring, although she wasn't touching it. Probably stuck, she thought practically, and then a revelation hit her. She wasn't dead! She didn't even seem to be hurt.

Cautiously, Vanessa glanced down at herself, half-expecting to see a mortal wound spurting blood. Dread bubbled through her, the first clear, sharp emotion she'd experienced since the crash. But there was no blood. She gingerly flexed her fingers, then dared to move her arms and legs. Elation surged through her. Everything was in working order. She was all right—she was more than all right! The burst of euphoria that rushed through her was unlike anything she'd ever experienced before.

And then the car door was flung open and a wild-eyed Lincoln Scott appeared before her. Vanessa blinked, unsure for a second if he was real or a recurrence of the vision she'd had moments before.

"My God, Vanessa, are you all right?" His voice was hoarse and thick.

She felt his hands on her, running over her arms, through her hair, tilting her head. His breathing was harsh and labored, as if he'd been working out. Or was in a state of sheer terror.

It proved to be the latter. "I followed you. I wanted to make sure you got home safely. I was a few cars behind you when I saw that idiot come at you on the exit ramp. I saw him hit you, I saw your car flip."

He was talking so fast, Vanessa had a little trouble following him. "I'm okay," she said in a voice that sounded as shaken as his. The adrenaline-induced euphoria abruptly faded and she came crashing down. Linc's panic seemed to be contagious. She caught it and retroactively experienced the wild and terrible fear which had been suppressed during the ordeal itself. She began to tremble.

"Sweetheart, I'm going to take you to the emergency room at the hospital. I don't think you have any serious injuries, but you should be examined anyway. You have a bump on your forehead and some bruises on your shoulder, probably from the shoulder harness. Thank God you were wearing it. If you'd been thrown through the windshield and out of the car . . ." Linc's voice trailed off and a deep shudder wracked him.

As he bent over her to fumble with the clasp of the seat belt, Vanessa touched her head to his shoulder. His clothes were wet, and she remembered them lying together on the terrace when the sky had opened up on them. She glanced through the door at the rain which was still pouring down. Linc, standing out in it, was getting drenched all over again.

Moving slowly, carefully, he lifted her out of the car. "It's all right, Vanessa. It's all over and you're all right," he said over and over in a litany to reassure them both.

The rain felt like cold, stinging needles as it hit her face, jarring Vanessa to full and frightening awareness of what had happened. And what had nearly happened. Her forehead felt sore and her shoulder and her chest were beginning to ache. She glanced from the smashed-up champagne-colored Ferrari Testarossa to Linc's face. He was grimacing and his blue eyes were filled with concern. His wet hair was plastered to his head and he was soaked through, but he seemed oblivious to the rain. He carried her swiftly, surely, to his car, a squat, bulbous-shaped candy apple red Pacer which was parked on the shoulder of the road.

"Lincoln," Vanessa whispered and clutched at his shirt with fingers that felt as if they'd turned to icicles. She burst into tears.

He deposited her in the front bucket seat of his car, then went around to the trunk and returned a moment later with a dark gray blanket. "I've always kept a first aid kit and a blanket in the trunk," he said, "but this is the first time I've ever had to use either of them."

He leaned inside to wrap the blanket around her. The coarse wool was scratchy and rough, but Vanessa clutched it as if it were the finest cashmere. She was crying and shivering and couldn't seem to stop.

"Vanessa, the truck driver who was behind you on the ramp witnessed the accident, too, and has radioed the police on his CB," Linc told her.

She glanced out the window and saw another man standing beside the car; he said a few words to Linc. She remembered seeing the lights of the truck behind her on the ramp, and with that memory came another, of the terror she'd felt when she realized that she had no escape from the oncoming car.

Linc climbed into the driver's seat beside her and

silently placed a box of tissues in her lap. "I—I can't seem to stop c-crying," she managed to choke out. It was difficult to talk and cry at the same time, and she was vexed with her tears that were falling as relentlessly as the rain outside.

"I n-never cry," she felt obliged to add. It was true, she'd never been one to resort to tears. The closest she'd come to crying as an adult had been when she'd learned that Troy Timmons, a man she had wanted to be more than a friend, was gay and would never hold the place she'd created in her daydreams for him. But even then she'd controlled herself and hadn't given in to tears. How she longed for a little of that rigid self-control now, as the tears continued to stream involuntarily from her eyes.

"You have a right to cry. That fantastic car of yours is a smashed-up wreck and this old heap doesn't have a scratch on it." Linc's voice was soft and gently teasing. "There's no justice on the roads," he added with a wry shake of his head.

Vanessa thought of all the wisecracks she'd made about his car, all the uncharitable and petty thoughts she'd had about it, and cried harder. The small car was spotless and well kept, she noted through her tears. Maybe Linc was as fond of it as her brothers were of their exotic sports cars. And she had made fun of it! It was bright red, she reflected, a rather dashing color for a somber actuary. Maybe Linc had always wanted a sporty car and choosing the candy red color was as close as he'd been able to come to his dream.

The thought set her off in a fresh bout of tears. "It's not an old heap!" she sobbed. "I love this car."

"I think you're getting hysterical," Linc said dryly and drew her into his arms, no mean feat as the gear console was between the bucket seats. "Nobody loves this car. I hate it myself. Its the car that won't die and I can't justify getting rid of it while it's still in perfect shape."

"You're being so nice to me and I was so bitchy

about your car." Vanessa gave a miserable little sniff. "I don't deserve it."

"Vanessa, what you didn't deserve was to be hit by some drunken idiot in flagrant violation of the law." His arms tightened possessively.

She closed her eyes and leaned against him. "I'm a mess," she said miserably. "I can't stop crying and I can't stop shaking. What's wrong with me? I don't usually fall apart like some kind of—of nervous weakling."

"There's nothing wrong with you, Vanessa. You've had a bad scare and the crying and shaking are very normal reactions. It's perfectly all right to feel both nervous and weak after what you've been through. Don't be so hard on yourself, honey."

"My brothers would be appalled if they knew how scared and weepy I've been acting. I never behave this way in front of them. They—"

"Vanessa, you shouldn't have to prove how tough you are to your own family. Families are supposed to offer support and comfort in times of stress. How can they do that if you insist on maintaing a façade of false bravado?"

"A Ramsey isn't weak," Vanessa said earnestly. "Daddy always says that we Ramseys cheerfully annihilate the weak and uncertain."

"Well, I don't," Linc said soothingly. "So you can be as weak and uncertain around me as you need to be. And I won't report you to your brothers," he added, stroking her wet hair with his hand.

She'd spent her life striving to be strong, proving she wasn't the weak little girl her parents seemed to expect her to be, afraid that if she gave in even once, she would be mired forever in a helpless, passive role. And now Lincoln Scott was granting her a license to be weak and she didn't feel threatened, only comforted, Vanessa reflected thoughtfully, as she luxuriated in the strength of his arms. It was a relief to cede control to someone else for a little while. *If that someone was Lincoln.* And only Lincoln. Somehow she knew that he wouldn't use her temporary weakness against her.

There was a knock at the window and Linc rolled it down. "Hey, Linc, the cops are here," said the truck driver.

"Thanks, Harry." Linc turned to Vanessa. "I'm going to talk to the police now, Vanessa. You stay here. I don't want you to go back out in the rain."

"How did you know the truck driver's name was Harry?" she asked quizzically, more interested in that fact than the arrival of the police.

Linc smiled. "We both were bemoaning the fate of that fabulous Ferrari Testarossa. Created an immediate male bond between us."

She smiled. And realized that she had stopped shivering and was no longer crying. How strange that allowing herself to be weak for a little while had enabled her to regain her strength. She pondered that as she watched Linc walk through the downpour to the police car, where Harry the trucker stood talking to the officer.

Linc brought the police officer over to the Pacer to interview Vanessa. While she answered the officer's questions, he made arrangements over Harry's CB to have her car towed. The he drove her to a nearby hospital where she was examined and X-rayed.

She had a swelling the size of a goose egg on her temple, but fortunately, there was no signs of concussion. The seat belt and shoulder harness had saved her from grievous injuries, but had inflicted long bruises from her shoulder to her abdomen from the force of keeping her in place. The doctor warned her that she would be sore for a few days and prescribed some analgesic tablets for the pain.

It was nearly two A.M. when she was finally released from the hospital. Linc had stayed with her the entire time and now he escorted her to his much-maligned Pacer, parked near the emergency ward's entrance. Vanessa slipped into the front seat, grateful to be out of the unceasing rain and even more thankful to be leaving the hospital with nothing more serious diagnosed than a few bumps and bruises.

She leaned her head against the back of the seat, closed her eyes, and sighed. Linc stared at her. She'd been quiet and subdued while talking to the police and to the doctors. The wet, bedraggled, and dispirited young woman sitting beside him bore little resemblance to the fiesty, regal goddess he'd been with at the party. The change in her saddened him. He knew he would rather have her ripping at him with her confidence intact than sitting bleakly and silently submissive beside him.

"I'll take you home now, Vanessa," he said quietly. "Can you give me directions from here?"

She reluctantly opened her eyes. "I live in River Oaks with my parents. At their insistence," she added with a faint trace of defiance. "My three older brothers moved into their own places right after they graduated from college, but Mama and Daddy go into hysterics anytime I mention moving out."

"I seem to recall a vintage quote along the lines of 'boys will be boys, but a girl must be a lady,' " Linc said with a smile.

Vanessa groaned. "Please, no vintage quotes. I've been through enough tonight." She lapsed into silence, speaking only when necessary to give Linc directions to her parents' home. It required too much effort to make even the most trivial small talk. The bump on her head was throbbing and it hurt even to think. Thankfully, Linc didn't seem to expect anything more from her than that she sit beside him and murmur a few words of direction at the appropriate times.

He was really quite comfortable to be with, she decided as she languidly watched the windshield wipers do battle against the driving rain. He didn't try to impress her by spouting an incessant stream of clever lines and he didn't expect her to entertain

him with a barrage of lively feminine chatter. She
was thankful for that.

And for his presence tonight. The thought of having to face the aftermath of the accident without
him made her shudder. He had handled everything,
taking much of the stress out of the highly stressful
situation.

"Linc, I'm really glad you followed me tonight," she
said softly. "I don't know what I'd've done if you
hadn't been with me."

"I'm glad I was there for you, Vanessa." He wanted
to add that from now on he would always be there
for her, but he didn't. The subject of Quentin
Ramsey's plans for their future together hadn't been
mentioned since they'd left the club, and he felt it
best not to resurrect the topic. Yet.

She took a deep breath. "Linc, what I did at the
club as we were leaving . . . asking Jody to get the
guards . . . making—er—unkind remarks about your
car . . ." She paused, searching for words. "It wasn't—
very nice."

Linc smiled to himself at her careful choice of
words. "No, it wasn't, Vanessa," he said blandly,
nodding his agreement. "In fact, it was downright
nasty."

It wasn't easy for her to admit being in the wrong,
and having her admission so swiftly seconded was
even harder to take. She straightened in her seat,
frowning. "But you must admit I had just cause."

"Why must I admit it?"

Her frown deepened and she turned slightly in her
seat. "Because it's true."

"What's true?"

"Is it me or is this conversation getting rather
hard to follow?" Her voice was stronger, sharper. A
surge of pink added color to her previously wan face
and her gray eyes began to flash.

"Probably because you hit your head," Linc said
solicitously. "Don't worry, you'll feel better after a
good night's sleep. The doctor said so."

"There's nothing wrong with my head," Vanessa said indignantly. "I'm thinking perfectly clearly. You're the one who's being dense. You refuse to admit I had grounds for my actions at the club this evening."

Linc flashed a sidelong grin. Gone was the glum little waif. In her place sat an imperious and affronted Vanessa Ramsey with all her fire. "What grounds?" he asked, biting back a laugh. He sounded maddeningly dense to his own ears.

Vanessa didn't see his grin or the teasing glint in his eye. But she heard his obtuse question and was appropriately maddened. "As if you didn't know! I had plenty of reasons for my *nasty* exit—your ridiculous assertion that my father tried to bribe you to marry me, for one."

"It's not a ridiculous assertion, it's the truth. You can ask him yourself when we get to your house."

"I am not waking up my parents at four o'clock in the morning to ask such a ludicrous question."

"It's two-twelve," Linc corrected her mildly.

Vanessa glowered at him. "I know what time it is. I was merely—"

"Exaggerating. For dramatic effect."

She folded her arms in front of her chest and scowled. "I've been trying to be gracious," she said, "but you make it incredibly difficult."

"Trying to be gracious." Linc mulled over that one. "I see. I thought you were trying to choke out an apology without admitting that you were actually apologizing. In fact, it seemed as if you were trying to lead me into apologizing to you."

"Well, you should!" spluttered Vanessa. "You made a heavy pass at me out on the terrace and—"

He interrupted her with a shout of laughter. "Honey, if I made a heavy pass, you were with me all the way."

Vanessa's body was one hot blush. She remembered far too well just how complete her response to him had been. "Lincoln Scott, you are—"

"Not a gentleman?" he supplied helpfully. "Follow-

ing the guidelines for standard banter, that seems
the obvious choice of phrase."

"I wasn't going to say that," snapped Vanessa.
"Because it gives you the perfect lead-in to tell me
that I'm not a lady. I know a little about standard
banter myself, Lincoln Scott."

"Then let's dispense with it. I think you're every
inch a lady, Vanessa."

She was caught totally off-guard by that one. "You
do?"

He nodded. "The most beautiful, spirited, passionate, exciting lady I've ever met."

"Oh." He'd rendered the insults she'd been about
to fling useless and irrelevant. "How do you do it?"
she asked, staring at him curiously. "How do you
manage to stay one step ahead of me all the time?"

"Ah, the wonders and mysteries of the actuarial
mind." He turned his head briefly to smile at her.

She felt her insides melt like warm sugar candy on
a ninety-degree day. His smile was an awesome
weapon, she conceded a little dizzily. How did one
keep her train of thought—let alone stay angry and
articulate—when he smiled in *that* certain way?

Things had truly changed since their introduction
earlier this evening, she reflected thoughtfully. Then
he'd been uptight, perhaps even a little in awe of
her. But now, now . . . her eyes slid over him and
she quivered with sexual awareness. He was the
essence of masculine confidence, and no wonder!
Her uninhibited physical response to him coupled
with her dependency and tears after the accident
had given him a power over her that no other man
had ever achieved.

If she weren't so tired, if her head weren't throbbing so much, Vanessa knew she would be alarmed.
She might even try to regain the upper hand. But
she couldn't seem to summon the energy for it at
this particular time, so she contented herself with
sitting quietly while Linc steered the car along the
highway.

A short while later, she directed him to the wide, tree-lined drive leading to the stately Ramsey mansion.

"Do you want me to come in with you to tell your parents about the accident?" Linc offered.

Vanessa shook her head. "I'll wait until morning to tell them. No sense waking them up at this hour," she glanced purposefully at her watch, "at *two-twenty-three*, when it's all over."

"Thank you for your accuracy," Linc said, amused. "When it comes to numbers, we actuaries are sticklers for precision."

A reluctant smile tugged at the corners of Vanessa's lips. "I'll keep that in mind when I'm exaggerating for dramatic effect."

He came around to open the door for her and they dashed together through the rain, seeking shelter under the roof of the wide front porch. Vanessa withdrew her key from her purse, then turned to Linc, who was watching her. Her heart did an odd little flip. Now that she was finally home, she found it hard to say good-bye to him.

"Linc, I—" she began, a slight tremor in her voice.

"Come closer and kiss me good night," he interrupted, watching her with intense blue eyes.

Her pulses launched into overdrive. "I most certainly will not!" She'd intended to sound haughty, but her breath caught in her throat, and the haughtiness somehow ended up sounding like breathless excitement.

"Why not?" Linc asked reasonably. "We know how much both of us would enjoy it."

"But why should I be the one to make the first move?" she demanded, then abruptly lapsed into appalled silence. She should have denied enjoying his kisses, not blurted out her thoughts like an inexperienced schoolgirl. And now she was blushing like one as well!

"Because I'm not going to lunge and grab you, much as I'd like to," Linc explained matter-of-factly.

"You're bruised from your shoulders to your waist and I don't want to risk hurting you." He held open his arms to her. "Come here, honey."

She stared at him. She couldn't believe that she was actually considering going to him. But she was. Perhaps that bump on her head was clouding her judgment, she rationalized. She took a tentative step toward him.

"You've been very supportive," she told him, taking another few steps. "And very, very helpful." A final step brought her directly in front of him. "I want to thank you for everything you've done for me tonight. And if the price of your help is a kiss, then . . ." She leaned over and quickly kissed his cheek. "Thank you, Lincoln," she said primly, "and good night."

Linc laughed softly as his arms came around her. "Nicely done, Vanessa."

"I thought so." She laid her hands on his chest. He was holding her lightly, in deference to her bruises. Vanessa knew a wanton urge to be crushed against him, regardless. She shivered.

"Cold?" Linc asked, slowly rubbing her back with his big, warm hands.

She shook her head no. She wasn't cold, despite her wet clothes and the cool night air. She arched against him, her breasts full and aching as they rubbed against the hard wall of his chest.

"Vanessa." Linc said her name raspily and his body was hard and taut from her sensuous movements. He felt his control beginning to slip. He cupped her nape with one hand and tilted her chin toward him with the other. Closing her eyes, she strained upward to meet his mouth.

Their lips met and clung and the heat and pleasure from the kiss swept rapidly through them both. His mouth moved and slanted over hers, seeking and finding the angle which would permit the deepest joining. When his tongue penetrated deeply, hotly, she rubbed it with hers, stoking the sensual fires which blazed between them to flash point.

As if reflecting the intensity of their passion, the sky simultaneously exploded with a fierce clap of thunder and a brilliant flare of lightning. A sudden gust of wind blew a shower of raindrops onto the porch, dousing them both.

The kiss ended abruptly and they stared at each other for a long moment, dazed by the force of their passion and the sharp, wet cessation of it. "We seem to have played this scene before," Linc said ruefully, casting a disparaging glance at the rain. "What is it with this storm? It appears to take a perverse delight in blasting us during our most—private moments."

"Maybe it's not the storm, maybe it's us," Vanessa suggested, still leaning comfortably against him. His arms were linked loosely around her waist. "Maybe we conjure it up somehow."

"If that's the case, we should take our act on the road. We could put an immediate end to the drought in the Southeast."

Vanessa chuckled. How strange to go from passion to humor without missing a beat. Yet she wasn't surprised that it should happen between her and Lincoln. The unexpected was becoming typical in her brief, volatile relationship with him.

They were pelted by another round of rain. Linc sighed and dropped his arms. "It's definitely time for you to go inside." He took her key and inserted it in the lock, then swung open the heavy wooden door.

Vanessa stepped into the spacious tiled entrance foyer. Her thoughts were tumbling around her mind in a disjointed swirl of confusion. When would she see him again? But she shouldn't see him again, not when he insisted on maintaining that crazy fiction about her father wanting him to marry her. But, oh dear heaven, she wanted to see him again!

Her mouth was warm and soft from his kiss, her body was aching and pliant from his caresses.

What should she say? What should she do? He knew exactly how he affected her, she thought wildly. No man had ever had that advantage over her before, no man had ever been sure where he stood with Vanessa Ramsey.

"Vanessa, take a hot shower and two of those pills the doctor gave you." Linc's voice filtered through the cloud of confusion in her mind. "And then go to bed and sleep late."

She cast a quick, covert glance at him. He was watching her, his lips curved into a sexy smile. Oh yes, he knew how he affected her, she thought, her heart pounding. He knew her mind was full of him, he knew her body was flushed and feverish because of him. The realization did not please her at all. She wanted to push him away as much as she wanted to pull him close. She'd never felt this way before. It was annoying, unnerving, it was insane.

"Good night, Vanessa," Linc called and raced down the porch steps and through the storm to his car.

He'd even had the last word, she mused. She should have been the one to send him on his way with a firm and succinct good-bye. Instead, she stood at the open door and watched the candy apple red Pacer travel along the length of the drive and disappear into the rainy night.

Five

_____

Vanessa's plans to sleep late were dashed when her parents burst into her bedroom at twenty to eight in the morning.

"Vanessa!" Nola Ramsey rushed to sit on the edge of her daughter's canopied bed, her wide hazel eyes round with worry. "Oh, my poor baby! An accident! Why didn't you tell us? The policeman said you were taken to the hospital! What—oh!" She spotted the swollen bruised wound on Vanessa's forehead and gasped. "My God! A head injury! Quent, we have to—"

Vanessa struggled to a sitting position, glanced at the clock and suppressed a groan. She felt groggy, whether from the effects of the pain pills or the lack of sleep or a combination of both, she wasn't sure. "Mama, I'm all right. Just a few bumps and bruises, that's all. I was released from the hospital after X-rays and a thorough examination. I'm fine, really." She stared at her mother, becoming more alert. "How did you find out about the accident? I planned to tell you when I woke up."

"The police called," Quentin Ramsey interjected, coming around the side of the bed to stare down at his daughter, concern apparent in his steely gray eyes. "They picked up the driver who hit you and wanted to verify your statement. I told them I was your father and demanded to know exactly what had happened."

"I'm sure you did, Daddy." Vanessa said dryly. It didn't take much imagination to picture Quentin Ramsey browbeating the hapless caller into divulging every detail in the police report.

"Darling, you should have called us!" exclaimed Nola. "When I think of my poor baby girl all alone out there in that rain last night, injured and terrified and—"

"Mama, you're overreacting. Linc was there and—"

"Who's Linc?" Nola interrupted.

"Lincoln Scott," put in Quentin. "So he was with you, eh?" A smile erased the anxiety from his face. "Well, thank the good Lord for that. I have every confidence in that young man."

"You know him?" It was Vanessa's turn to interrupt. She was very still as she studied her father's face.

Quentin cleared his throat. "Yes. I—um—we met through mutual business associates, and—er—I was quite impressed with the man."

Vanessa frowned. It was most unlike her father to stammer. And she noticed that he was avoiding meeting her eyes. *"Your father suggested that I sweep you off your feet. Somehow, I was supposed to make you fall madly in love with me tonight."* Linc's voice echoed in her ears. Her heart skipped a beat. No, his assertion was preposterous, she silently insisted. A novel approach he'd come up with to grab her attention.

But her father was taking great care to avoid her searching gaze. And he looked incredibly guilty.

"Well, I'm just relieved and grateful that this Lincoln Scott was there to help you, Vanessa," Nola said, breaking the silence. One glance at her mother's open face and clear hazel eyes convinced Vanessa that if Quentin Ramsey had hatched some plot, his wife was not aware of it.

"Nola, my dear, why don't we let Vanessa get some rest?" Quentin took his wife's arm and attempted to lead her from the beautifully decorated rose and cream bedroom. He cast a quick glance over his shoulder at his daughter. "Go back to sleep, princess. We're sorry to have burst in and awakened you."

Vanessa was no longer sleepy. "I'd like to talk to you, Daddy," she said, throwing back the covers and climbing out of bed. She was wearing an oversized blue silk nightshirt which came to her knees. "About Lincoln Scott."

Nola's interest was instantly piqued. "Is he a nice boy, Vanessa? Handsome? When did you meet him? This is the first time I've heard you speak of him."

"He's not a boy, Nola, he's thirty years old, and every inch a man," Quentin interjected. "And I would certainly call him handsome. Good all-American looks. Strong jaw, good teeth, fine head of hair. Good eyes, too. Doesn't wear glasses. And he's intelligent. Has a mind like the proverbial steel trap. Good stock, Lincoln Scott."

"Good stock? Quent, you sound as if you're describing a stallion for breeding purposes," Nola admonished with a chuckle. She smiled at her daughter. "I'd much rather hear your description of him, honey."

Vanessa was frowning fiercely at her father. *Breeding purposes?* He was edging toward the door, clearly intent on making a quick escape. "Daddy," she began in a dangerous tone.

"I have some phone calls to make, pumpkin. I'll talk to you later." Quentin was gone in a flash.

"Mother, I have every reason to believe that Daddy is involved in something truly outrageous." Vanessa's heart was pounding. Her father's behavior was giving her definite cause for alarm. He was acting guilty and he was trying to avoid discussing Lincoln Scott with her. Why? That was the question that made her stomach feel as if it were on a bumpy airplane flight.

"So what else is new?" Nola laughed fondly. "Now, tell me all about your young man, darling."

"Mother, you're not taking me seriously. And Linc's

not my young man, he's just someone I met last night." She had no desire to endure an eager inquisition on the subject of Lincoln Scott. "If you'll excuse me, I'm going to take a shower and get dressed." She headed into the tiled bathroom adjoining her bedroom suite.

An hour later, Vanessa went downstairs to join her parents on the screened terrace for breakfast. She wore a white long-sleeved jersey under her bright yellow cotton knit tank dress to cover the bruises on her shoulders and arms. She didn't feel up to facing the exclamation of horror they were sure to draw.

"Ah, here she comes now," Quentin boomed jovially, and Vanessa stopped dead on the threshold and stared.

Lincoln Scott was seated at the round glass table with her mother and father. He rose to his feet at the sight of her.

Vanessa's gaze flicked over him, unwillingly noting how well his khaki slacks and khaki shirt fit his hard muscular frame. Her eyes lifted to his face and she suffered a momentary jolt at the sight of his deep blue eyes and rugged features, the thatch of thick blond hair. He looked like a golden sun god as he stood on the bright, sun-washed terrace. She swallowed.

"Good morning, Vanessa."

It annoyed her that he was the first to speak. She should have had that privilege. And the way her pulses were racing at the sight of him, the way her stomach was doing flips . . . The whole situation was suddenly intolerable to her. "What are you doing here, Lincoln?" she asked coldly.

"Vanessa, that's no way to talk to the man who saved your life last night," Nola admonished disapprovingly. "Lincoln was concerned and considerate enough to stop by this morning to inquire as to your condition. I should think that you would at least show him the courtesy of—"

"Mother, I'll admit that he was helpful, but he

hardly saved my life." Vanessa threw Linc a fierce glare. "And I thanked him last night."

"Yes, she did," Linc interrupted calmly, holding her eyes with his. "Most graciously, I might add."

Vanessa saw the glint in his eye and knew he was remembering that hot, deep kiss on the front porch. And though her parents might be fooled into thinking that his smile was benignly polite, Vanessa saw the pure masculine challenge in it. Her blood took fire. "If you've come seeking a monetary reward for your services, Mr. Scott, I'm quite willing to write you a check for whatever amount you feel entitled to."

"Vanessa!" Quentin exclaimed, frowning at her. "I want you to apologize to Linc. He came here this morning at my invitation because I wanted to thank him personally for taking care of you last night. I will not stand for you insulting a guest in our home."

"Did you want to thank him or get a progress report, Daddy?" Vanessa marched over to the table, gray flames burning in her eyes. "Is it true that you made Lincoln Scott some sort of—of offer to marry me?"

She had the satisfaction of seeing both her parents temporarily stunned into speechlessness. An incredulous Nola stared from Quentin to Lincoln, her mouth agape. Quentin Ramsey, looking distinctly uncomfortable, turned his attention to twisting his cloth napkin into a tight cylinder. Only Linc remained cool and calm and utterly collected. He grinned at Vanessa, as if the two of them shared a hilarious private joke.

"What kind of an offer did you make, dear?" Nola recovered enough to ask.

Her mother's response said it all, Vanessa thought grimly. Nola Ramsey wasn't shocked or angered that her husband would resort to such an odious scheme. And she would stand behind him all the way, just as she always did. Vanessa fought a hurtful sense of betrayal. Why should she have expected anything different? she asked herself. When had her mother ever stood up to the male Ramseys on her daughter's behalf?

Quentin cleared his throat. Clearly, he had not expected to be confronted by his daughter on this matter. He shot Linc a baleful glance. "Exactly what did you tell her?"

"You mean *why* did he tell me, don't you, Daddy?" Vanessa snapped. Oh God, It was true then, everything Linc had said last night, what she hadn't allowed herself to believe. Her father had commissioned a perfect stranger and offered him God-only-knew-what to marry her.

"I told Vanessa last night that I would always be honest with her," Linc said matter-of-factly. "I don't want any lies or deceptions standing between us." He turned intense blue eyes onto Vanessa. "I want to marry you, Vanessa. I told you that last night, too."

"Oh, we're going to have a wedding!" Nola rhapsodized with a sigh. "Vanessa, Lincoln, I'm so happy for you both."

"Mother, how can you say that?" howled Vanessa. She'd expected her mother to back up her father, but her dewy-eyed romanticism was a little too much. A lot too much! "Lincoln Scott wants to marry me because Daddy is bribing him to do it. What's the payoff?" she demanded, wheeling on her father. "I'd at least like to know my going price."

"This isn't going at all like I planned," Quentin muttered.

"Why, Daddy? Why? How could you?" Vanessa felt hot tears prick her eyes and furiously blinked them back. Disillusionment, betrayal, fury, and pain coursed through her, so mixed together that she couldn't begin to separate one from the other.

"How could I?" Quentin stood up and faced his daughter. "Why? Because I love you, Vanessa. Because I want you to be happy and healthy and safe."

"I'm all those things now," Vanessa raged. "You didn't have to—to try to buy me a husband to achieve that!"

Quentin shook his head. "No, you're not safe, not anymore. Haven't you been reading the papers? Listening to the news? Well, I have. And what I've been hearing has alarmed me more than anything has in years. Everyone who's not in a committed monogamous relationship with someone they've known a long, long time is at risk. When a man or a woman sleeps with someone, they're also sleeping with every person that person has slept with for the past five to seven years."

"Daddy, for heaven's sakes, you sound like the Surgeon General's report. What's all that got to do with me?"

"Aha, I was right." Quentin pounded the glass table with his fist. It rattled ominously. "You're ignoring the threat, not taking it seriously. You have no concept of how far-reaching, how encompassing this crisis actually is. That's why it's up to me to protect you, Vanessa."

"Protect me from—from getting AIDS?" Vanessa was incredulous. "You want to marry me off to Lincoln Scott to save me from AIDS? Mama, I think it's finally happened. Daddy's lost his mind."

"Quentin, dear, that does sound rather—er—extreme," said Nola rather anxiously.

"AIDS is getting all the headlines, but there are other serious sexual diseases out there as well," Quentin said soberly. "I've never been one to avoid unpleasantness, to bury my head in the sand and hope that a problem will go away. And when it involved a threat to my little girl's safety, I knew I had to take action. A group of my friends and I were talking about the situation, and one of them made the remark that not even all our money could keep our kids safe from the threat of AIDS. And that's when I got to thinking—the hell it can't! I can use my money to find my baby girl a man who poses no threat to her health, a man who'll remove her from the dangers of—"

Vanessa clutched her head with her hands. "I can't

believe I'm hearing this! Daddy, what makes you think that Lincoln Scott is such a virus-free white knight? How do you know who he's been sleeping with for the past five to seven years?"

Quentin smiled a feral smile. "I know because I had him investigated in intimate detail."

That was a bit too much even for Nola. She grimaced. "Oh, Quentin!"

Vanessa's eyes flew to Linc's face. "It's true," he said dryly. "I thought I'd spare you the—uh—intimate details of the investigation."

"No, Linc, my boy, perhaps it's best that she know." Quentin clapped him heartily on the back. "I'm proud and honored to have you as my son-in-law, Lincoln. Your kind of safe sexual background is a distinct advantage in today's precarious social scene."

"Does that mean you're a virgin, Lincoln?" taunted Vanessa. "Chaste and untouched?"

"Well, no. But the next best thing," Quentin interjected happily. "He's had only two sexual relationships spanning the last ten years. Both were monogamous, long-term, and consecutive, of course. Furthermore, he was the first sexual partner for both those young women. It took me a long time to find him, but find him I did. A handsome, intelligent young man of good character with a safe sexual history. The perfect matrimonial candidate for my little princess."

"You sound as if you're making a marketing pitch for one of the Ramsey malls—the best that money can buy!" Vanessa was horrified, incensed, and embarrassed. She couldn't look at Lincoln or her parents. "It's absurd, it's disgusting. I won't do it, *Quentin Ramsey*! I will not marry Lincoln Scott."

"Vanessa, dear." Her mother moved to her side and put a maternal arm around her shoulders. "Why don't we table this discussion until after you've eaten breakfast? Come, sit down, I'll pour you a nice, hot cup of coffee. We have your favorite—fresh strawberries and cream."

"Mother, I can't think of food at a time like this!"

"Hey, I can think of Maria's *jamón y huevos* at any time! I asked her to whip me up a batch." All heads turned to Jed Ramsey who came bounding onto the terrace wearing nautical whites and deck shoes. "Good morning, Mom, Dad." He planted a smacking kiss on his mother's cheek and nodded to his father. "I stopped by to pick up the keys for the boat on my way to the marina. I'm spending the day on the water with Tammy Kay," he added with an unmistakably lascivious grin.

"Who's Tammy Kay, dear?" asked Nola.

"Has Dad investigated her sexual history?" Vanessa demanded.

"Her *what*?" Jed sat down at the table, poured himself a glass of orange juice and a cup of coffee, then helped himself to a dish of strawberries. His mother reached over to sugar the berries for him.

"Is Tammy Kay a virgin, Jed?" Vanessa asked sharply.

Jed nearly choked on his juice. "Good Lord, I hope not!"

"Then what about her previous lovers? You'd better hope there've been only one or two—who were virgins before hopping into the sack with Tammy." She shot her father a scathing look. "Isn't that right, Daddy?"

Jed looked up from his berries to stare at his sister. "Vanessa, does that Easter egg–size lump on your head have something to do with the weird questions you're asking?"

"Vanessa, do sit down and eat a nourishing breakfast like your brother," urged Nola. "And, Jed, you haven't even bothered to ask how your little sister happened to get that nasty bump on her head."

Jed shrugged. "I figure someone came after her with a baseball bat. I've had the urge to do it many times, but never got lucky enough to clobber her." He spotted Linc, who'd remained standing in silence, watching the family byplay. He stretched out his arm, offering Linc his hand to shake. "I'm Jed Ramsey. I take it you're one of Vanessa's latest victims? Let me give you a piece of friendly advice: Run, don't walk away from the girl while you're still able." He capped his friendly advice with a chorus of "Maneater," sounding lamentably unlike Hall or Oates.

"I'm Lincoln Scott," Linc said easily, smiling as he shook Ted's hand. "Vanessa's fiancée."

The normally unflappable Jed dropped his juice glass. It hit the stone floor, sending bits of shattered crystal and orange juice splashing in all directions.

"Oh my, we'll have to get this cleaned up right away before anyone gets cut. Conchita!" Nola called for the maid as she bustled into the house, appearing extraordinarily relieved to do so.

"Vanessa's fiancée?" Jed gasped. He stared at his sister, clearly stunned by the news. "But how? When? Hell's bells, Vanessa, I didn't even know you were dating anyone seriously!"

Vanessa balled her fingers into fists and squeezed till her knuckles turned white. Jed was the most relentlessly caustic of her brothers, with a memory as precise as a computer bank's. He remembered—and loved to relate, preferably in public—every and any foolish and embarrassing thing that had ever happened to her. If he were to learn the truth about this fiasco . . .

Her insides were churning, burning; she felt her throat close. He would torment her endlessly for years—in front of the family and all their friends. He would delight in making her the laughingstock of Houston. She knew Jed, he was merciless, and he loved to needle her until she was bleeding from the pricks. He'd always been after her, from the day their mother had carried her, the precious little bundle wrapped in pink, home from the hospital. Vanessa had heard the story of how five-year-old Jed had accidentally upset her bassinet, dumping his newborn sister onto the floor three hours after her arrival home. Fortunately, there had been a plush carpet and she hadn't been injured. But she'd always been certain that it hadn't been an accident at all, just a declaration of the sibling war which they'd been waging for years.

No, Jed must never know that their father had attempted to bribe a "sexually safe" man into marrying her, Vanessa decided, tilting her chin with pure Ramsey determination. Deceiving him for a while would make this mortifying situation even more bizarre, but she really had no choice.

"I'd never confide anything about anyone I was seriously involved with to you, Jed," she said with what she hoped was her usual sisterly acerbic tone. "You'd take it upon yourself to scare him away." She forced herself to walk around the table and stand beside Linc. "I did warn Linc that I had a cretin for a brother, but he said he'd learn to live with it."

Linc slipped his arm around Vanessa's waist and pulled her close. She stiffened, but when she saw that Jed was staring at them, open-mouthed, she willed herself to relax. She'd straighten Lincoln Scott out later, she promised herself, smiling up at him.

Her eyes were as cold as diamonds on ice, Linc thought. He assessed the situation instantly. Vanessa didn't want her brother Jed to know about her father's part in their "engagement" and was willing to play the role of loving fiancée to divert him from the truth. Taking full advantage, he touched his lips to hers. They were cool and soft and desire, as sharp as a razor, sliced through him.

His hand moved to her nape and he lightly stroked the sensitive skin there. Her scent filled his nostrils, that exotic, elusive perfume which he knew would always call forth evocative, sensory memories of her.

Vanessa felt a pulsing warmth blossoming deep within her. He was so close that she could feel his body heat emanating from his hard frame. The touch of his fingers seemed to be softening her bones to butter. A cursory glance down her body showed her nipples tautly outlined against the thin double layer of cotton, and a surge of hot color turned her cheeks crimson. It was happening again, just like last night, she wailed in silent despair. Her volatile and voluptuous response to Lincoln Scott wasn't a never-to-be-repeated fluke; the fire he'd lighted in her body last night continued to burn unabated.

A wild rush of conflicting emotions whirled through her. She wanted to be alone with Linc, she wanted to twine herself around him, to open her mouth on his and feel his muscles pressing sensuously against her. On the other hand, she wanted to dump the big ceramic bowl of strawberries over his head and tell him exactly what she thought of his mercenary collusion with her father. And then—then, she would treat her wicked brother Jed to a coffee stain on his pristine white pants.

"But who is he, Vanessa? What does he do? Where's he from?"

Jed's voice drew her out of her somewhat contradictory fantasy. She moved away from Linc and he quickly sat down on one of the chairs, but not before she saw undisguisable evidence of her own sensual effect on him. Her heart thumped. Knowing that she was capable of arousing him with the same degree of speed and intensity with which he aroused her was an added stimulation in itself. She picked up a piece of the morning paper and began to fan herself with it. The last thing she needed was added stimulus.

"Linc is originally from Kansas and he heads his own actuarial firm here in Houston, Jed," Quentin spoke up when neither Vanessa nor Linc seemed inclined to answer Jed's question. "And it just so happens that I've hired him to design and implement a pension plan for the entire company. Of course he'll handle the administration of the plan as well as all the taxes."

So that was the payoff, Vanessa divined, her gray eyes snapping. She was to be sold for a crummy pension plan? She wondered who was more despicable—her father for offering, or Linc for accepting? Perhaps it was a loathsome draw.

"A lucrative account," Jed said, eyeing Linc coolly. "Ramsey & Sons has thousands of employees. I can guess who talked Dad into signing on with your firm."

Vanessa stared. "You can?"

Jed gave a short laugh. "Vanessa, I've been watching you twist Dad around your little finger for the past twenty-five years. I know damn well that it wasn't his idea to suddenly draft a pension plan for the entire company. You decided that your new boyfriend ought to get a piece of the action, you batted those big eyes of yours and maybe whined a little and bang! Lincoln Scott is suddenly aboard the Ramsey gravy train."

Vanessa chuckled. She couldn't help it. Her so-smart big brother had gotten it backward! She was incredibly relieved. "You're an idiot, Jed." She flashed him a maddeningly smug, brother-baiting smile.

"No, *he's* the idiot." Jed pointed his thumb at Linc. "You don't know what you're getting into, buddy. It might look like a good deal to you now, but marrying her ain't gonna be no day at the beach. Are you sure you want to give up your freedom, your peace of mind, your sanity for a few thousand pension plans?"

"Lincoln is well aware that if he marries me for money, he can expect to earn every cent." Vanessa smiled at Linc, then at Jed. "Slowly and painfully," she added with chilling sweetness.

"Money doesn't enter into it," Linc said gallantly. "I wanted Vanessa from the moment I saw her."

Vanessa was grateful to him for the lie. If her brother swallowed it, she was spared a lifetime of humiliation.

Jed merely shrugged. "It's your funeral, man," he said to Linc.

"Such talk!" Quentin inserted himself into the conversation. Having studied the interaction between his son and daughter, he now knew how Vanessa wanted the scene played. And of course, he would indulge his darling princess's wishes. "This is a love match between Vanessa and Linc, of course. Why, I've been bursting with the news, but these two lovebirds swore me to secrecy. They wanted to break the news themselves when they felt the time was right. Which is their privilege, of course."

Vanessa wondered if Jed suspected that their father was spinning a fairy tale. Knowing her brother's opinion of her, he probably found it impossible to believe that any man could love and want to marry her. She sat down at the table and spooned some of the strawberries into a dish. Had she ever outfoxed Jed? The answer was a resounding no. She'd better remove herself from the spotlight and divert the attention from Linc . . .

"Now you can focus all your attention on Jed's risky single state, Daddy." She gave her most winning princess smile. "I mean, from what I've been reading, a single man can't be too careful these days. Take this Tammy Kay person you're undoubtedly planning to sleep with on the boat today, Jed. Do you realize that you're not only sleeping with her, but with every man she's slept with for the past five to seven years? I'll bet that number is somewhere into the hundreds, knowing your trashy taste in women."

Linc swallowed a laugh. Vanessa was playing the role of bratty little sister to the hilt and he enjoyed her performance, while sympathizing with her older brother. But he underestimated the effects her words would have on Quentin Ramsey.

The older man had visibly paled. "I've been so worried about my little girl that I've hardly had a chance to take proper care of my boy—not that I haven't been equally concerned about him." He sighed. "I'm not going to draw an easy breath until all my children are in safe, committed relationships."

"Well, now you can give Jed's marital status your

full concentration, can't you, Daddy?" Vanessa asked softly.

"I'm gonna kill her," Jed muttered, slamming his coffee cup into the saucer. Miraculously, it didn't break. He jumped to his feet. "So help me, Vanessa, I'm—"

"Daddy, wouldn't Tara Brady be the ideal match for Jed?" Vanessa suggested blithely. "Such a sweet, virginal ingenue." She turned simperingly to Linc. "Tara is the younger sister of Shavonne and Erin who are married to my brothers Slade and Rad. Two sisters married to two brothers, isn't that sweet? And sort of karmic, too. Wouldn't it be just *peachy* if somehow Tara and Jed got together? Then we'd have three sisters married to three brothers." Her eyelashes fluttered. "So romantic."

Jed didn't appear to think so. "No!" he roared, smacking his fist into his palm as he paced the floor in a frenzy. "I absolutely, positively refuse to consider it! Dammit, I won't have anyone plan my life for me! I make my own decisions, my own choices."

"Not in this family you don't," Vanessa murmured.

"You're a troublemaking little viper!" Jed glowered at her. "Oh, Vanessa, I'll get you for this! I'll—"

"You don't have to go berserk," she interrupted mildly. "It was just a suggestion."

"And a mighty good one, too, pumpkin." Quentin reached over and patted her hand. "Jed, can't you see how concerned your little sister is about you? She just wants to be sure that you're safe and in these times, one can't be too careful." His face darkened. "And, Jed, I just remembered that I need you to fly to Sun City, Idaho, with me today to check on a construction site for our new mall there. Vanessa, why don't you and Lincoln take the boat out? It's supposed to be a beautiful sunny day, perfect for boating."

"Dad, I'm taking the boat! I have a date!" Jed shouted.

"In my company, a vice-president's job takes precedence over some frivolous outing," thundered Quentin. "So if you deserve your position, if you're man enough for it, Jonathan Edward Ramsey, you'll fly to Idaho, where your presence is needed."

"Maybe we should think of giving Linc the position of vice-president, Daddy," said Vanessa, her voice convincingly earnest. "We know how admirably ambitious *he* is. Why, he stops at nothing when it comes to advancing himself."

Only Linc seemed aware that the fiery challenge in her eyes completely belied the innocent sincerity in her tone. His hand snaked out to circle her waist and she glared at him. He smiled. She smoldered.

She jerked in her chair when she felt Linc's leg brush hers under the table. It felt hard and warm and strong. He hooked his ankle around hers and drew it between his legs. "Behave, Vanessa," he warned in a low voice, his blue eyes dancing with laughter. She tried unobtrusively to free herself. He didn't relinquish his grip on her.

Jed was too infuriated to notice any of it. "I can't take this!" he exploded. "Just because *she*'s managed to trap some poor sucker doesn't mean that I have to be condemned to a similar fate!"

"Enough of this." Quentin stood up. "Come on, son, our plane leaves in forty minutes. Vanessa, Linc, enjoy yourselves on the water today." He leaned down and kissed the top of Vanessa's head and shook Linc's hand heartily. Then he strode from the porch, a furious Jed following in his wake.

"Poor Jed," drawled Linc. "He was all set to spend his Saturday on a boat with a hot date and then Vanessa speaks and he's headed for a construction site in Idaho."

Vanessa jerked her hand free, disengaged her leg from his and stood up. "A construction site in Idaho is a paradise compared to where I'd like to send you!"

Linc grinned. "Is that any way for one lovebird to talk to another?"

"Just in case you're too dense—or too conceited—to realize it, that little charade was strictly for Jed's benefit. If he were to find out about your disgusting little deal with Daddy, he'd—I'd—" she broke off, scowling. "I want you to leave immediately, Lincoln Scott. I can't tolerate another second of your revolting presence."

"We're spending the day together, Vanessa," Linc said, his voice pleasant and calm and totally at variance with the implacable determination in his blue eyes. "I don't know the first thing about boating, so if you'd rather not do that, it's fine with me. But we're going to do something, somewhere together. It can be your choice or mine, that's negotiable, but we're going to be together. That's not negotiable."

"Who are you to tell me what's negotiable and what's not?" Vanessa raged, temper darkening her eyes. She was hardly aware that her fingers had wrapped around the handle of a delicate china pitcher, half-filled with cream, until she followed Linc's gaze down to it.

"Don't even think it," he advised quietly.

Fury flashed through her with high-voltage intensity. She'd been trying to break her lifelong habit of throwing things, having decided that it was childish and unbecoming. Watching her sisters-in-law curb her small nieces' impulses to pick up and hurl had been something of an eye-opener to her. Why, Vanessa wondered, hadn't her parents ever stopped her from throwing whatever breakable item was on hand while she was in a fit of temper? Over the years she'd broken more glass than the proverbial bull in a china shop. Last year she'd decided on her own that she simply had to stop and she'd managed to do just that.

Until now. Her fingers ached as she recalled the thrill of heaving a missile at its target, the satisfaction of observing its crash landing. And Lincoln Scott's warning was something akin to waving a red flag in front of the bull who'd shattered all that china. How dare he tell her what to do—and in her own home! She lifted the small pitcher and drew back her arm.

"I'll catch it, "Linc warned. "I was the first baseman from Little League through high school and I seldom missed a ball. And after I catch it, I'll carry you out to my car and take you to my apartment where you'll learn a whole new way of handling frustration."

Heat scorched through her. His sensual threat should have enraged her further, but it wasn't rage that coursed through her as she visualized herself alone with him in his apartment. Vanessa's breath caught in her throat. It was sexual excitement, it was physical hunger. It was passion. The pitcher slipped through her suddenly nerveless fingers and crashed to the floor.

Linc started toward her and Vanessa instinctively began to back away. "I didn't throw it," she said hastily. "It—it dropped."

He continued his advance and she continued to retreat, their gazes locked together. He stretched out his arms and caught her, his big hands settling on her waist and kneading gently, sensuously while he drew her to him.

"It's not like I have to stand here and meekly submit to this," Vanessa told him breathlessly, as her body made contact with his. He was hot and hard and she shivered. "I've been educated in the martial arts. I could take your arm off if I wanted to. I could yell so loudly I'd shatter every glass on the table. I—I could even shatter the table!"

"I think we've had enough broken glass around here this morning," Linc said, skimming his lips over hers with just the tip of his tongue emerging to tease and entice.

The breath that Vanessa had been holding escaped on a muffled moan. Her arms slipped around his neck.

Six

His mouth opened over hers, warm and lazy, as his lips leisurely caressed and rubbed hers. She tasted him as his tongue slipped into her mouth and she arched into him, suddenly moist and dizzy with passion. Her heart drummed wildly in her ears as his hands moved over her with a possessive demand that made her forget everything but the desire, the need, to meet and fulfill those demands—and to make her own on him.

She melted against him, feeling soft and pliant and more feminine than she had ever felt in her life. His virility enhanced and glorified her femininity in a way she had never dreamed possible. The passion engulfing them both was honest and real. In Linc's arms, there was no room for one-upmanship and sexual strategies, there were no winners and losers, but equal partners, giving, taking, pleasuring . . .

With a low, sexy growl, Linc's mouth left hers to kiss her neck with a hungry ardor that made her moan. "I want you, Vanessa. I want you so much I'm half crazy with it," he said raspily, and she clung to him, her breasts pressing against his hard chest.

His hands cupped the softness of her bottom and he lifted and fitted her to the cradle of his thighs. When he rubbed against her intimately, her mind spun wildly out of control, and she cried out his name.

Her implicit surrender plunged Linc into a dizzying vortex of passion where time and place were irrelevant. There were only the two of them, each wanting, each needing . . .

He slipped his hand between their bodies and lifted her skirt.

Vanessa felt the soft cotton smooth upward, felt his big, warm hand on her bare thigh and went weak. She wanted, she ached . . .

Both heard the sound of the approaching voices long before either was capable of distinguishing who was speaking. Linc and Vanessa sprang apart, flushed and shaken, before Nola and the maid, Conchita, joined them on the terrace.

"Oh dear!" Nola spotted the remains of the china creamer before she noticed Vanessa and Linc, who'd collapsed onto two cushioned armchairs positioned opposite each other. "The Limoges." She shrugged. "Oh well, Vanessa threw the matching sugarbowl at Jed a couple of years ago. I suppose it's time to order a new set."

Conchita frowned at the mess of juice and cream and crystal and china on the stone floor and lapsed into a torrent of impassioned Spanish.

Nola turned to her daughter. "Vanessa, Daddy tells me that you and Lincoln are taking the boat out today. Such a marvelous day for it, hmm?"

Vanessa raised stricken eyes to Linc. He was watching her intently, his pupils dilated from the intensity of their passion, his lips slightly swollen from the ardent hunger of their kisses. He looked virile and sexy and she closed her eyes against the force of the feelings flowing through her. Were her eyes and her lips exhibiting similar signs of those tempestuous moments when she had thrown all caution and restraint and control away and allowed him to—

Deeply shaken, she quickly turned away from him. He'd had his hand under her skirt right here on the terrace with her mother and the household staff not far away. She remembered the feel of his palms gliding along her thighs and her heart seemed to stop and then start again with a jolt. His fingertips had brushed the silk of her panties and then—

And then they'd heard her mother and Conchita coming to join them! What an unexpected shock that had been! Vanessa felt poised between nervous laughter and tears.

"Vanessa, are you all right, dear?" Nola sounded concerned. "Is your head hurting you? Perhaps you shouldn't go out today, after all. You were injured last night and—"

"I'm fine, Mama, Vanessa said quickly. She couldn't stay home and have her mother hovering and fretting over her, she had to get away. "I want to go boating today."

She cast a quick, covert look at Linc. He seemed to be as dazed as she felt, and she found consolation in that. Consolation and a certain triumph. "Lincoln doesn't know a thing about boating, but of course, I know all there is to know about it, so there'll be no problem," she heard herself say, sounding surprisingly like her old, confident self.

Quite suddenly she felt reckless and giddy and positively high on the adrenaline pouring through her veins.

"Will you be home for dinner?" Nola asked. "I've invited Erin and Shavonne and the children over because Rad and Slade will be in Idaho with Daddy and Jed until late tonight." She beamed at Linc. "I can't wait for you to meet my darling daughters-in-law and my four adorable grandchildren."

"I'll think we'll pass on dinner, Mother," Vanessa inserted hastily. She wasn't about to go through another performance for the rest of the family.

Nola looked disappointed. "Well, some other time then."

"Yes, some other time," echoed Vanessa, rising to her feet and hurrying from the terrace.

Linc was right behind her.

"Some other time on some other planet in some other lifetime," she spat at him.

"Are you sure you know how to handle a boat?" he asked doubtfully, diverting her completely from the subject of dinner with her family.

"Of course I do! I insisted on learning everything that my brothers were taught about boating." She glanced sharply at him. "Why, you're afraid to go, aren't you? Coming from a land-locked state like Kansas, you're scared to take a boat into the Gulf." The notion exhilarated her. On the boat on the water, *she* would have complete control and power. And she needed that, especially after this morning's display of Linc's awesome sexual power over her.

Linc cleared his throat. "Well, if you're sure . . . and if you insist on taking the boat—"

"I do insist!" In her glee to prove her nautical superiority, she forgot that she'd had no intention of spending the day with him. It wasn't until they were on their way to the marina that the possibility that he may have outsmarted her occurred to her.

She cast him a quick, sharp glance. He was driving one of her father's cars, a sporty white Aston Martin Volante convertible. She'd found the thought of arriving at the marina in his trusty old Pacer intolerable and insisted on taking one of the cars from the Ramsey fleet. Linc's admiring glances at the Volante had struck a chord in her. Her father and brothers were acutely car-mad, and she'd always carefully followed their lead. She guessed that Lincoln Scott had never been behind the wheel of an ultra-expensive car, and the masculine appreciation in his deep, blue eyes as he gazed at the Volante told her that he'd like to. On impulse, she'd casually tossed him the keys. "You drive. I don't feel like it today."

The sun was shining, the sky blue and clear, the temperature pleasant in the high sixties. The warm wind blew through her hair which she'd tied back with a colorful silk scarf.

"This car is great!" Linc said with an appreciative sigh, running one hand reverentially along the steering wheel. "Thanks for giving me the chance to drive it, Vanessa."

His blue eyes were alight with enthusiasm. She withheld the nasty crack she was about to make concerning his ambitions to marry money and drive rich men's cars. Something about a man's little-boy excitement over a terrific car always managed to evoke an affectionately sentimental reaction from her.

But Lincoln Scott didn't deserve such a response, she reminded herself crossly. He'd agreed to her father's bloodless plan to marry her—for the chance to design and implement a pension plan for Ramsey & Sons! She mustn't ever lose sight of that fact.

Linc followed her abroad the Ramsey's custom-built cabin cruiser, named the *Ramsey Queen*, admiring the graceful lines of the boat while admiring even more the slender, graceful curves of Vanessa's figure.

Vanessa turned abruptly and found his eyes dwelling hungrily upon her. He didn't look at all like a man afraid to go to sea. "You tricked me," she said accusingly. "You're not scared to go out on the boat."

"True, I'm not. Not with you at the helm," he added, probably as a sop, Vanessa thought, annoyed with herself. Here they were, just the two of them, falling in with her father's plans. And Linc's. They were going to spend the day together, that point wasn't negotiable, he'd said. Vanessa frowned. Worst of all he had been smart enough to let her stumble into his trap all on her own.

"I have great faith in your abilities as a captain, Vanessa." Linc smiled at her, a sexy smile, a friendly smile as if he were her friend and her lover.

Vanessa fought the urge to return that smile. He was neither, she admonished herself. He was a money-grubbing opportunist, eager to use her for his own financial advancement.

"I'll give you a quick tour of the boat," she said coolly. She pointed out the compact but fully equipped kitchen and bath, the long, narrow cabin with three sets of bunk beds lining the walls. "The boat sleeps eight. When we were younger, we used to take overnight trips and my brothers and I would sleep in the bunks. We haven't done that for years and years," she added a little wistfully.

She showed him the wood-paneled lounge with its carved mahogany bar and cushioned leather stools and wall of shelves holding assorted games. "And here's the main cabin." She opened the door to a luxurious cabin where a large porthole placed strategically near an oversized bed provided a stunning view of the water. A sofa, chair, and table were arranged in a cozy alcove on the other side of the cabin.

"This is obviously where your brother Jed planned to entertain his date," Linc said, pointing to the bouquet of fresh flowers and a bottle of champagne chilling in an ice bucket.

"The manager here at the marina is very accommodating. Jed must have placed his order in advance." She blushed suddenly. "Don't get any ideas about taking advantage of this setup. You're here strictly for a boat ride."

When Linc made no comment, she turned to glare at him fiercely. "I mean it, Lincoln. I'm not going to bed with you."

His blue eyes sparkled with deviltry. "I understand your wanting to wait until we're married, darling. I respect you for it."

"I'm thinking of taking you far out into the Gulf, throwing you overboard, and abandoning you to the sharks," she warned as she tramped back to the deck. Linc followed and watched her at the control panel as she turned the key in the ignition. The engine spluttered to life.

"Good plan," he said dryly. "You can tell the authorities it was an accident and pretend to be distraught. There won't even be an investigation."

Vanessa suppressed a grin. "Come here and mind the throttle while I cast off the stern and the bow lines," she ordered, raising her voice over the noise of the idling motor. She knew he was watching her cast off and was pleased that she pulled it off without a hitch. Fortunately, the skirt of her dress was full and allowed her sufficient freedom of movement, but she wished she hadn't raced out of the house without taking time to change into slacks, especially when a warm gust of wind sent her skirt whipping to her hips. She beat it down with both hands, her cheeks flushed as she observed Linc's interested and amused reaction.

Scowling, she took over the wheel, nudging him aside. "Don't you even have the sense to be afraid of a woman with homicidal fantasies about you?" she demanded, resuming their verbal joust.

"The fantasies you have about me match the ones I have about you." He wrapped his arms around her waist and she felt the long hard length of him against her. "Hot." His lips skimmed the slender length of her neck. "Sexy." His hands inched upward with excruciating slowness to rest just under her breasts. "And exciting." He flicked his thumbs over the rigid crests and Vanessa sucked in her breath as an arrow of pure fire pierced her belly. "And, no, they don't scare me, Vanessa."

"Let me go, you idiot!" she said shakily, slipping away from him into the captain's seat. "Do you want me to wreck the boat?" She thrust the throttle forward and the engine roared and surged with power. The cruiser cut through the blue-green water with increasing speed.

Linc stayed close to her, shifting one arm to her waist, while his other hand rested possessively on her shoulder. His fingers delved below the cotton neckline of her jersey to explore last night's bruises.

America's most popular, most compelling romance novels...

Here, at last...love stories that really involve you! Fresh, finely crafted novels with story lines so believable you'll feel you're actually living them! Characters you can relate to...exciting places to visit...unexpected plot twists...all in all, exciting romances that satisfy your mind and delight your heart.

EXAMINE 6 LOVESWEPT NOVELS FOR

15 Days FREE!

To introduce you to this fabulous service, you'll get six brand-new Loveswept releases not yet in the bookstores. These six exciting new titles are yours to examine for 15 days without obligation to buy. Keep them if you wish for just $12.50 plus postage and handling and any applicable sales tax.

☐ **YES,** please send me six new romances for a 15-day FREE examination. If I keep them, I will pay just $12.50 (that's six books for the price of five) plus postage and handling and any applicable sales tax and you will enter my name on your preferred customer list to receive all six new Loveswept novels published each month *before* they are released to the bookstores—always on the same 15-day free examination basis.

40311

Name_____

Address_____

City_____

State_____Zip_____

My Guarantee: I am never required to buy any shipment unless I wish. I may preview each shipment for 15 days. If I don't want it, I simply return the shipment within 15 days and owe nothing for it.

R6234

When he placed his lips on the delicate line of her collarbone, she immediately jerked away.

"You know, my father is all wrong about you. Sexually inexperienced—*ha*! You're fast, Lincoln Scott. You're smooth. You know all the right moves." And she was responding to his slightest touch with heart-stopping fervor.

Linc settled back in the comfortable seat beside her, still within touching distance. "Not being promiscuous doesn't equal sexual inexperience, Vanessa. I've often thought that those slick bed-hoppers are more interested in quantity than quality."

"Oh, and you guarantee quality lovemaking? Do you have written affidavits from the two lovers in your committed, monogamous, long-term serial relationships—damn, listen to me, I sound like Dr. Joyce Brothers," Vanessa broke off with a scowl. She was horrified to realize that she was hating the thought of Linc in a long-term sexual relationship with another woman. And he'd had two of them. Meaningful, committed. Didn't that mean he'd been in love with each of them? She was suddenly enraged.

She steered the boat into the rough wake of another cruiser and cursed as they were bounced and jolted and splashed by the waves. She should have avoided it. Had she been thinking clearly, she would have. Her temper rose.

"If you're so terrific in bed, and if you're so into commitment and monogamy, why didn't you marry either of your sexually safe lovers?" She felt a crimson heat sweep through her. "They were both virgins, according to Daddy. Is that a requirement of yours?"

"Your father has the answers to all those questions and more in his dossier on me. Why not ask to read it?"

Vanessa eyed him sharply. He didn't sound as cool or dry or affable as he usually did. He sounded— irritated. So she had struck a nerve? She silently cheered. "You don't like the idea of Daddy having a dossier on you?" she taunted.

"What do you think? For heaven's sake, Vanessa, your father's gumshoe found out everything there is to know about me right down to the name of my high school trig teacher and breed of the family dog. Do you actually think I like knowing that my whole life is an open book to Quentin Ramsey?"

Vanessa arched her brows. "So what breed is Spot, anyway?"

"A good old all-American mutt." Linc reached out to wind one of her long, dark tresses around his finger. "But your question about why I haven't married is a valid one. I dated Julia for six years and Karen for nearly three, but I guess marriage simply wasn't in the cards."

Vanessa resorted to Ramsey-style needling. "Because their fathers weren't millionaires?"

"I met Julia in college and we stayed together for three and a half years after graduation—the romance had long gone and we'd become a comfortable, convenient habit with each other by the time we mutually decided to call it quits. We're still fond of each other—she invited me to her wedding and I went as an old, close friend."

He paused and shrugged. "A year later I met Karen. In the beginning, things were great, but she came to resent my financial contributions to my family. It was a constant bone of contention between us and in the end was responsible for breaking us up."

"She dumped you because you insisted on bailing out the family on the good old farm in Kansas?"

"Something like that. Karen was an accountant at the insurance firm where I worked and she kept a careful ledger of every cent I sent to my family. She felt she was being deprived of what was rightfully hers, and the thought of me continuing to contribute to their support after we were married was intolerable to her. I found the thought of letting my family down equally intolerable. In the end we argued all the time."

"One of those bitter breakups," Vanessa said. "I assume Karen isn't going to invite her old buddy Linc to her wedding?"

Linc grimaced wryly. "Not hardly. So there you have it—a capsule version of my romantic history. I may not have a little black book filled with the names of my conquests, but I assure you that I'm not sexually inexperienced. What about you?"

She turned the wheel abruptly to the right and the boat lurched. Linc went sliding along the seat away from her. "Why not ask Melinda Sue Harper or Lexie Madison about me? I'm sure they'll give you an earful."

"I'm asking you, Vanessa."

"Well, it's none of your business."

"Oh, I see. The double standard is alive and well in the Ramsey family. You get the story of my past, but I'm not even supposed to ask about yours."

"Exactly. My father didn't have a dossier on me, did he?" Every muscle in her body tensed.

"No," Linc said quietly. "Other than expressing his displeasure with your choice of companions and his fear of you remaining single, your father told me nothing about your love life. I did hear something from that tell-all gossip maven, Melinda Sue, though."

"About Troy Timmons, no doubt. Melinda Sue positively relishes that tale." Vanessa stared stonily ahead.

"Were you in love with him?"

"I never had a chance to find out. I was attracted to him and I certainly pursued him. I liked being with Troy—he was one of the few men I've ever known who actually talked to me as if I were a person and didn't treat me like a prize to be grabbed. That's why after I found out he was gay, I still wanted him as a friend." She smiled slightly. "Troy likes me very much now that I'm no longer chasing him. I suppose I used to threat *him* as a prize to be grabbed. Now we treat each other as fellow human beings and have a friendship that I value. We spend time together whenever I'm in New York."

"You can call him tonight and tell him that we're getting married," Linc said with a definite trace of masculine possessiveness. "Invite him to the wedding. I'd like to meet your old friends."

"Does that mean you intend to invite your good pal Julia?" she snapped.

"I thought I would, yes."

"I don't know which offends me more." She was seething. "Your arrogant assumption that we're getting married or your cavalier suggestion that *old friends*—which is nothing but a pallid euphemism for old flames—ought to be invited to the wedding. Well you can forget both." She glowered at him. "*If* I were getting married—which I'm not—I would absolutely refuse to have any of the groom's ex-lovers as guests, no matter how buddy-buddy they'd remained."

"Even one old flame is one too many?" Linc suggested amiably.

"Yes!"

He smiled. "If I didn't know any better, I'd think you were jealous, Vanessa."

"Me?" Her voice seemed to be stuck in her throat and barely squeaked out. "Jealous of you?"

He shrugged. "Just a thought. Okay, I won't invite Julia and her husband to our wedding, but how do you feel about keeping them on our Christmas card list?"

She laughed, much to her consternation. And then scolded herself for not maintaining stricter control of her impulses. "You're outrageous," she told him, striving for severity. The last thing this man needed was encouragement.

"Fortunately, you've been raised with outrageous men in an outrageous family. You've learned how to cope. After spending your life dealing with your father and brothers, a man like me should be easy for you to handle."

She shot him a dry glance. "I might have thought so yesterday, but now I'm not so sure. For example, when I fight with Daddy and my brothers, words fly and china flies and nothing is ever resolved. When I fight with you, you manage to twist things around so we aren't fighting anymore, and I'm not angry anymore, and I'm never really certain how you've done it." Her voice trailed off and she frowned thoughtfully. His style was far more insidious; slipping beneath her anger and making her laugh, making her like him. Added to that was the powerful sexual attraction she felt for him. She swallowed hard. Things were going too far too fast; she was getting in too deep and she knew it, yet she couldn't seem to halt the inexorable progression. Nothing she said or did seemed to put Linc off. Worse, she wasn't sure anymore if she really wanted to put him off.

"Your father mentioned that you worked for Ramsey & Sons, but he didn't say in what capacity. What kind of work do you do for the company, Vanessa?"

His adept, abrupt change of subject jerked her off balance yet again. He seemed to be extraordinarily skilled at it and she knew she should resent it, yet she found herself marveling at his perception instead. After this morning's revelations, she needed to vent her frustrations about the Ramsey stranglehold on her life. How clever of Linc to give her a way to do so without involving himself and the issue of marriage.

She found herself pouring out the whole story of her captivity at Ramsey & Sons. Linc listened carefully, saying nothing until she'd finished outlining her restlessness and unhappiness.

And then he said bluntly, "I think you should quit."

She stared at him. "And spend all my time on the social circuit?"

"No, open your own office as an interior designer. Compete with other space planning firms. If Ramsey

& Sons hires you, fine, but it would be as an autonomous businesswoman."

"You make it all sound so simple. Don't you think I haven't wanted to strike out on my own? Mama and Daddy just freaked at the thought of me out there in the big, bad business world. You've seen how my father overreacts to what he perceives as a threat to me. And his reaction to what he perceives as a threat to Mama is even more extreme."

"And your being independent and on your own is viewed as a threat to your mother?"

Vanessa nodded. "It's crazy, I know. They're ridiculously overprotective. And as tempted as I am to leave Houston and live my own life, I know it would break my parents' hearts so I just can't bring myself to do it. They're maddening and controlling but . . ." She shrugged, staring out at the vast blue-green waters.

"They're your parents and you love them," Linc finished. "I understand. I know the power and force of family loyalty."

Vanessa thought of his breakup with the aforementioned Karen because his family needed his financial support and she had objected to it. "I guess you do."

"As far as families go, we have much in common, Vanessa. Both of us suffer from a little too much adoration. My family depends on me and looks on me as their hero and savior for keeping them financially afloat. Your family treats you like a frivolous, pampered pet. Both are opposite sides of the same coin."

"Well, I could use a little less adoration and a lot more freedom."

He smiled. "If I promise to temper my adoration of you and to try not to run your life, will you promise to temper your adoration of me and not be overly dependent on me? To hold the hero worship?"

Vanessa laughed. "That's an easy promise to make."

The sound of another boat's motor drew her attention and she steered the *Ramsey Queen* out of its path. A family—father, mother, and several children—was on board. Both craft sped on their way after exchanging friendly waves and horn blasts. The sea breeze was cool and refreshing as the sun shone down upon them. Vanessa glanced at Linc, who smiled at her. She felt relaxed and content, which was odd because relaxation and contentment did not come easily to an intense and driven personality such as hers.

And then it occurred to her that she was suddenly ravenously hungry. They had been speeding through the water for quite some time. "Do you want to have lunch?" she asked.

"Sounds good. There was a lot of food around your breakfast table this morning but not much of it got eaten."

She pulled the throttle back and put the motor in neutral. The boat slowly came to a stop and rocked in the calm waters. "Always a hazard when dining with the Ramseys. Sparring is so much more interesting than eating."

Linc shook his head. "No wonder you're so skinny."

"Skinny?" She assumed an affronted air. "The word is sleek—or chic. Slender is acceptable, and even thin will do. But skinny? Never." She went to the bow where the anchor was attached to a coil of nylon cable.

"I stand corrected. Let me help you with that anchor." He rolled up the sleeves of his shirt to his elbows, exposing the rippling muscles of his forearms.

Vanessa stared at the blond hair covering his bare arms, saw the power in those whipcord muscles, and swallowed hard. His hands were big, the palms rough. He looked strong, like a man accustomed to hard, physical labor—the result of growing up on a farm, no doubt. His strength, his masculinity tempted and beckoned.

She instinctively fought against it. She was no weak, feminine nitwit bowled over by manly muscles. "I don't need any help," she insisted stubbornly and picked up the anchor. "I can do it myself."

She proceeded to throw out the anchor, then turned to face him in triumph. Actually, it was the first time she'd ever anchored the boat alone, such a task having been deemed "man's work" by the Ramseys. Now she'd finally had her chance and had succeeded!

Linc found her victorious smile particularly appealing. He couldn't resist her. "You're a first-rate sailor, Vanessa," he assured her, catching her around the waist.

"Let me go, you big—"

With one lithe movement, he turned her around to face him. He held her against him.

"Big—" His eyes, as dark and deep blue as the sea captured hers and her thoughts seemed to fragment. Yes, he was big. And hard and strong and— She caught her breath on a gasp. A fire had begun to burn in her belly, spreading its heat upward to her breasts and lower to the secret softness between her thighs.

She stopped struggling, forgetting that she was angry with him, forgetting everything but the hot, fierce excitement streaking through her. He was hard and aroused and she could feel the shape of him pushing against her.

"I want to make love to you, Vanessa," he murmured against her ear, then made her shiver as he traced the delicate shell with his tongue.

Vanessa moaned. It was all too sudden. "Linc, no," she whispered. The wind blew up her skirt again and she felt the touch of his hand on her thigh. She gasped.

He stroked the sensitive skin with his fingers, gliding back and forth with sensual lightness, drawing heat and wetness from her in passionate response. "I've never felt this way about any woman before," he said, his voice husky and sexy and as arousing as his caresses. "You affect me like a nuclear meltdown—I only have to be near you and I burn up."

She made a sound that was a strangled mixture of a laugh and a moan. "That's the way you affect me, too. It's—It's scary," she admitted shakily. The usual Vanessa Ramsey policy of admitting to no fear or weakness didn't hold when it came to Lincoln Scott, she acknowledged achingly. When she was in his arms, when he was touching her, she was as honest and open and vulnerable as she'd ever been in her life.

"Don't be afraid of me, honey. I won't hurt you," he said soothingly as his clever fingers made her squirm mindlessly with pleasure.

"Won't hurt me?" Her breathing was ragged and her voice emerged as a half sob. She wanted him with frightening need, yet she couldn't forget the situation between them. "You don't think it hurts knowing that you intend to cold-bloodedly marry me for money?"

He slowly withdrew his hand, then wrapped his arms around her, holding her in a hard, tight embrace. "Suppose I refuse your father's offer to design and implement the pension plans for Ramsey & Sons? And suppose I agree to sign whatever type of ironclad prenuptial agreement that you and your lawyers dream up? Then will you let me love you, Vanessa? Will you marry me?"

Seven

Shocked, Vanessa drew back and stared at Linc. "You'd marry me without the pension plan deal? And with a prenuptial contract? But why? What would be in it for you then?"

"Spoken like a true Ramsey." Linc gave her a slight shake. "*You* would be what's in it for me, you little idiot."

"But we hardly know each other."

"The length of time we've known each other is irrelevant. I'm not one for making rash and impulsive decisions—on the contrary, I've been criticized for lacking spontaneity more times than I can count. But I trust my instincts, Vanessa. There is a bond between us. It's inexplicable and intangible, but it's real. From the moment we met, I knew you were the woman I've been waiting for my entire life."

Vanessa felt sudden tears blur her eyes and decided that she was a silly, sentimental fool. She, who viewed herself as an expert on masculine lines and approaches, was thrilling to this one. Because she so desperately wanted it to be true? "You sound like the cover blurb on a romance novel. The so-called bond between us is based solely on sex," she mocked huskily. "I won't deny that there's an explosive chemistry between us. I don't really understand it, but—"

"There's no reason to denigrate a strong sexual attraction," he interrupted.

"There's no reason to marry because of it, either."

"I want more than an affair with you, Vanessa."

"How about a *relationship*, then? You're quite good at those, hmm?" She thought about his past with Julia and Karen and felt herself grow decidedly hostile. "We could have a committed, monogamous relationship. I'd be number three in the series. And since I'd be with you—the man my father has already had certified as sexually safe—he can hardly complain."

Linc stared down at her for a long moment, then clasped his hand around her nape. "I think it's time for lunch. There's no point in trying to carry on any kind of discussion when we're both sexually frustrated *and* starving for food."

"Lincoln, it's not that easy to—"

"Yes." He silenced her by running one long finger along the shape of her lips. "It is that easy. Now let's eat."

She heaved an impatient sigh. "If I weren't so hungry, I'd insist on finishing this ridiculous argument. And winning it! Because sexual passion, no matter how volatile and exciting, is hardly a—"

He leaned down and gave her a swift, hard kiss. "If you keep talking about volatile and exciting sexual passion, you're going to wind up in bed, not in the galley, sweetheart. Keep that in mind."

Dazed, more than a little besotted, she followed him to the galley below.

She had crowded into this space with her brothers any number of times without noticing how incredibly cramped the quarters were, she thought. Linc's muscular frame dwarfed their surroundings. She couldn't seem to move without some part of her touching some part of him. Why did she have to be so aware of him? So *sexually* aware. It was just what she'd been trying to tell him a few minutes ago, she thought. The esoteric bond which he claimed existed between them was sex. Pure sex. Powerful, mind-numbing, body-tingling, and irresistible sex.

Her legs felt unaccountably shaky and she leaned against the cabinets for support.

She tried to concentrate on transferring the food from the refrigerator to the counter top. Sliced ham, turkey, roast beef. Potato salad, lettuce and tomatoes. Her gaze slid to Linc who stood watching her, one hand braced against the narrow door jamb. "Stop looking at me that way," she said sternly, adding some Swiss and cheddar cheeses to the selection of food.

"What way?" he asked, amused.

"As if you'd rather devour me than this." She pointed to the food.

He laughed. "Oh, baby, don't tempt me."

"I won't dignify that with a response," she said airily with a haughty toss of her head. After placing the bread and condiments on the counter, she added fruit and small iced cakes for dessert.

"Jed planned quite a feast for himself and his girlfriend," Linc observed. "Do you suppose his date will forgive him for standing her up?"

"If he wants her to, she will. Jed has an uncommon ability to talk his women into doing exactly what he wants."

"Wish I had that talent. Do you think he'd let me in on his secret?"

"You just stay away from my brother Jed. He'd be a terrible influence on you. Anyway," she looked at him from beneath her lashes, "you seem to do pretty well when it comes to getting what you want from women."

"I'm only interested in one woman, Vanessa. And that's you."

"Yes, you are into serial monogamy, aren't you? That's what made you so invaluable to Daddy."

He narrowed his brows thoughtfully. "You're really pushing me, honey. Why, I wonder?"

"I'm trying to push you away," she retorted. "Lunch is served."

They ate out on the deck. Vanessa was surprised

at how easily conversation flowed between them. They both loved to read, although their tastes in books were remarkably dissimilar. She mocked his choice of dry nonfiction and he teased her about her preference for blood-and-gore spy thrillers. There were a few books—bestsellers in a number of categories—that they both had read and they debated their differing opinions on them.

"We have absolutely nothing in common," Vanessa remarked with a laugh as she reached for a vanilla cake iced with butter cream frosting and fresh strawberries.

"You're wrong, honey, we have quite a bit in common although it might not be immediately apparent. But look beyond our superficial differences. It hardly matters that our reading tastes differ. What counts is that we both spend hours of our spare time reading. And our values are remarkably similar, which is far more important than having identical interests."

"Similar values?"

"Values are the things that people believe in and hold worthy," he explained patiently.

She shot him a speaking glance. "I know what values are. I just don't see how ours can be remotely similar. You grew up on a working farm and I was raised like a princess in the city."

"The financial status of our respective families is irrelevant to our sense of family, Vanessa, the sense of family which we both share. We each have tremendous feelings of loyalty to our families and we understand those feelings in each other. If sharing interests isn't a prerequisite for a good marriage, sharing values is."

"Now *you* sound like Dr. Joyce Brothers," Vanessa grumbled.

Linc laughed. "And we can make each other laugh. Humor is the universal antidote for marital tension, Vanessa."

"Oh, our marriage would be a joke, all right."

He gave her scarf a tug and her hair tumbled loose around her shoulders. "Always have to have the last word, hmm?"

He was smiling at her in a way that made her breath catch in her throat. He was different from any man she'd ever met, and their little spats had yet to escalate into the battle of egos she always seemed to engage in with other men. Linc didn't view her sarcasm as threatening, he had too much self-confidence. And he wasn't of an argumentative, competitive bent, so he didn't always feel the need to jump into a quarrel and win.

"You're impossible," she accused, but it came out sounding more like an endearment instead.

"You like impossible people," Linc said easily. "They remind you of you."

She snatched back her scarf, fighting a grin.

"So what's next on the agenda?" asked Linc as he began to gather up the remains of their lunch. Vanessa watched him and then followed him down to the galley where he proceeded to finish the cleanup. "Do we speed around some more or what?"

"If it were a littler warmer we could swim. And if I didn't hate fishing we could fish. I suppose we could sunbathe on the deck." The yawn she'd been attempting to suppress escaped. She stole a quick glance at Linc, hoping he hadn't noticed.

He had. "Ah, at last. My cue to suggest a nap."

Her lips twitched. "I'm not going to bed with you, Linc."

"Neither of us got much sleep last night. And you have that knot on your head and all those bruises. You need to get some rest, Vanessa."

"Your concern for my welfare is touching," she said dryly. "And I repeat—I am not going to sleep with you, Linc."

"Will you go to bed alone? And sleep alone?" He smiled at her. "There are quite a few beds on this boat."

"That's true. I could sleep in one of the bunks."

"And I'll sleep in one of the others."

"No way, mister," she said sternly. "I'll sleep in one cabin and you can have the other. I want the cabin with the bunks—you can have Jed's lair."

"Okay," he agreed amiably.

"And get rid of the flowers and champagne," she ordered. She wasn't sure why, but she did not want him sleeping amid those seduction props.

"Your wish is my command," he drawled.

She laughed, she couldn't help it. His tone, his expression were so droll. They both knew she was barking out orders like a Marine drill sergeant, but he found her amusing, not offensive. Once again she admired his ability not to be overpowered by her. "I only want to lie down for a half hour or so," she said. "Then we'll go back to the marina."

"Pleasant dreams," Linc said and kissed her mouth lightly.

Touching her lips with the tips of her fingers, she watched him walk off in the direction of the big cabin.

Vanessa's dreams were not conventionally, benignly pleasant. They were erotic, hot and wild and strong. And starred Lincoln Scott. She awakened abruptly, her heart pounding in rhythm to the pulsing throb deep within her. She lay still and stared around her, her eyes wide.

The dream had seemed so real. A surge of color suffused her cheeks. She was slightly stunned—and embarrassed—by its intensity. She'd dreamed Linc had been kissing her, touching her, and she had been moaning and aching for more. Even now, as she lay in the narrow bunk in the empty cabin, her body felt taut and restless, burgeoning with intense and unfulfilled desire.

Swinging her legs over the side of the bunk, she got up and walked stealthily to the other cabin, opening the door a crack to peek inside. Linc was laying on his stomach in the middle of the bed, sound asleep. There were no signs of the flowers and champagne, and she smiled to herself. Acting on pure impulse, she slipped inside.

She didn't allow herself to think. Rational thought ran a poor second to the primitive, yearning hunger which drove her to stand beside the bed. She stared down at him. He was breathing deeply, evenly. Vanessa tried to pace her own breathing to his, to no avail. Her breath was coming in short, shallow gulps and her pulses were thundering in her ears. She sat down on the edge of the bed.

"Linc." She laid her hand on his shoulder, wondering vaguely what had gotten into her. Was she still under the spell of her dream? She'd awakened feeling sultry and wanton and vibrantly sensual. And empty and aching.

Linc opened one eye. He came awake instantly, leaping from deep sleep to alertness without a second's gap. Vanessa was sitting beside him on the bed, her hand on his shoulder. She didn't realize that he was awake yet and he took advantage of the fact to study her. Her pearl-gray eyes were enormous and she nervously ran the tip of her tongue over her lips in unconscious provocation. He felt his body begin to tighten.

Vanessa drew back her hand and stood up. The shaft of sunlight pouring through the porthole rendered her thin cotton dress almost transparent and he studied the fine lines of her body underneath the soft material. The thrust of her small breasts, the narrow waist and gentle slope of her hips, her firmly rounded derriere. Hard with wanting, he sucked in a sharp breath.

As if in a dream, he heard the disembodied voice of Quentin Ramsey echoing in his head. *You're a man of strength and action and character, Linc. The ideal mate for my daughter. I want you to have her, she's yours.*

A man of character. Linc tensed. Would a man of character do what he was about to do? Did a man of strength feel as if his blood were on fire whenever he gazed at the woman he wanted? The woman he would have, he added firmly. With lightning speed, he stretched out his arm to capture her hand with his. Whatever else he may or may not be, he was definitely a man of action.

"Oh!" Vanessa jumped a little. "You startled me I—I didn't know you were awake."

His fingers closed warmly around hers and he sat up. "I was hoping I wasn't dreaming." He pulled her slowly, inexorably toward him. "But you're really here."

She flushed. After all her insistence about not sleeping with him, it was ironic that she'd been the one to creep into his bedroom. Ironic and embarrassing. Vanessa braced herself for the zinger that would make him the undisputed winner in this round of one-upmanship.

Instead Linc lifted her hand to his mouth and pressed his lips to her palm. "You're so beautiful, Vanessa," he said softly, "and I want you so much."

She went weak inside. "Oh, Linc," she whispered. Her knees seemed to buckle and she sank down onto the edge of the bed.

She could never remember feeling this way in her life. Her skin was tingling and her muscles seemed to have liquefied. A melting heaviness had settled in her abdomen. She didn't realize that she had reached for him until she felt his hard, tanned cheek beneath her hand.

He hooked his hand around her nape and slowly drew her mouth to his. Her dark lashes fluttered shut and she emitted a small sigh as his mouth closed over hers. Soft and pliant, her lips parted to welcome the swift thrust of his tongue. It teased hers, playing havoc with her senses, enticing with quick, elusive darts, then plunging deep to rub and stroke.

"You taste so good," he murmured, kissing his way along the slender curve of her neck before claiming her mouth again. "Ah, Vanessa, you're so soft and warm and sweet."

Vanessa's response was to lock her hands behind his neck and pull him closer. She ran her hands over the hard muscles of his shoulders, reveling in his strength.

Their kiss deepened and lengthened, becoming more intimate, the passion building to incendiary levels. His palm covered one breast and she shivered and arched against his hand.

He lowered her to a reclining position on the bed and her whole body tightened when he slid his thigh between hers. Her eyelids languidly drifted open and she stared into the burning blue depths of his eyes. What she saw there made heat sear her every nerve. Passion. Intensity. Dark-eyed sexual intent. He wanted her and he was going to have her. Vanessa quivered.

Their gazes locked, he slowly, purposefully traced the outline of her nipples with a lazy finger, circling first one, then the other, over and over again until they were taut and achingly sensitized. A moan escaped from her throat and she twisted sinuously, arching toward him.

His hands cupped her, lifting and learning the soft weight while his thumbs caressed her nipples which were tight and straining against the cloth in a sensuous bid for more attention.

"You're perfect," he murmured. "So responsive. So lovely." He pressed his face into the rounded softness, breathing in her scent. "Oh, Vanessa, you feel so good."

His lips closed around first one distended nipple, then the other, and Vanessa cried out as a spear of erotic pleasure pierced deeply into her womb, releasing a flood of liquid heat. His tongue dampened the material, heightening the luxuriant sensuality of his kisses. The force of her emotions thrilled her but alarmed her too.

Linc felt her tense. "Sweetheart, what is it?" he asked softly, stroking her breasts, adoring the way they fit his hands, loving their sweet softness. Though he felt as if he were charged with sensual electricity and wanted nothing more than to release it deeply inside her, he wanted her equal and eager anticipation. He was too emotionally attuned to her to ignore her sudden and unexpected high-strung edginess.

Vanessa gave a shaky little laugh. "I was just thinking that it's almost too late to turn back. Too late to change my mind. M-Maybe it already is."

To her relief, he wasn't annoyed with her sudden doubts. His smile was intimate and affectionate. "Weren't there song lyrics along those lines? 'Too late to turn back, too late to change my mind'?"

"Too late to worry," Vanessa added and gulped.

"But you are worried," he said quietly. "Why, Vanessa?"

She searched her mind for a plausible explanation, anything but the truth. "Well, it's—uh—it's the pension plan for Ramsey & Sons. If Daddy wants one drawn up for the company, I don't see why you shouldn't be the one to do it, regardless of whatever happens between you and me."

"You were thinking of a pension plan while I was making love to you?" He grimaced. "Who's the actuary here, anyway?"

Vanessa suppressed a groan. She was doing a stellar job of making a fool of herself. "It's just that I want you to have the contract with no strings attached." She really did, she realized, she wanted to help him in any way that she could. "I mean, with the family farm in jeopardy you—"

"Honey, I appreciate your sentiments, but I've never felt less like talking about the farm in my life. Or about pensions." He caught her chin between his fingers and tilted it upward, forcing her to meet his deep blue gaze. "Tell me what's really bothering you, Vanessa."

She stared deeply into his eyes. "You have to swear that you'll never tell a soul as long as you live. Especially not my brothers." Her lower lip jutted mutinously. "Or my father, either, dammit."

"I promise. You can trust me, Vanessa."

"Ha! Famous last words. I bet Brutus said them to Caesar while he was polishing his dagger."

"I like your imagery," Linc said dryly. "Very phallic. But what can't you risk telling me?"

She lay rigid, staring at the ceiling. "If I tell you, you'll have enough ammunition to zap me for the next twenty years."

He stroked her hair gently, lazily, as if they had all the time in the world. "Honey, this may come as a surprise to you but not all people view confidences—or mistakes or moments of weakness—as ammunition to hold over another. That seems to be a uniquely Ramsey trait. One I don't care to emulate."

"Never mind, Linc." She sat up. "Let's just say I've changed my mind about making love and leave it at that. I'm going to take the boat back now."

Linc stared at her. Her back was ramrod straight, but her hands were trembling. He thought back on her responses to him which had been hot and quick and almost helpless—as if she were a stranger to her own passion. She was edgy and high-strung, wanting him, yet fighting it. As if she were both nervous and aroused at the same time and to the same intense degree. Linc's logical mind added up the facts and weighed the conclusion. Fear? Or inexperience?

He sat up and put his hands on her shoulders. She didn't seem like a woman who had been sexually frightened—which left the unlikely choice of sexual inexperience. It seemed impossible. How could Vanessa Ramsey, a notorious man-eater and balls-buster—a self-proclaimed one!—be inexperienced with the opposite sex?

Linc frowned thoughtfully. Although he hadn't known her long, he had gained some important insights into her character. She had a strong sense of self-esteem, an indomitable pride. And hadn't she admitted that the stories about her were exaggerated, that she was actually quite controlled? That was not a likely portrait of a blithely promiscuous playgirl.

He felt the tension in her muscles and kneaded them with strong fingers, moving from her shoulders to her neck. There was one more salient factor to consider. She'd been deeply aroused by his love-making; he was sure she'd been as passionately hungry for him as he had been for her. Yet she'd cut it off, just like that. He knew she had to be enduring the same sexual frustration as he, yet she'd accepted it . . . because she wasn't aware that there was an alternative to the condition? Because she'd never known sexual fulfillment? A woman experienced in the pleasures of sex wouldn't have found it so easy to deprive herself of the gratification she knew awaited her.

The clues added up. Inexperienced and a stranger to sexual satisfaction. She was operating under sheer virginal control. "Vanessa," he said quietly, continuing to massage her tight muscles. "You're a virgin, aren't you?"

Vanessa jerked spasmodically and tried to pull away from him. But Linc had anticipated just such a reaction from her. He held on to her, dropping one hand to her waist to pull her against him and securely anchor her there.

"Let me go, you snooping, prying, gossip-monger!"

"I take it that's a yes answer?"

"Go ahead, laugh! I knew you would! Who could resist howling with laughter? Such rich irony. Vanessa Ramsey, the vamp, villainess, vixen is a virgin."

"Good alliteration," Linc said approvingly. "But why should I laugh at you?"

She turned her head to stare at him, certain that he was mocking her further. The action brought her lips within inches of his. His blue eyes were intent and serious; he was studying her. And he wasn't laughing.

"Because I'm a fraud," she whispered. "And you found me out."

"You're not a fraud, just an extremely private person, Vanessa. Oh, you give the impression of being the ultimate extrovert, very open and blasé, but you're not that at all. You're guarded and deeply reserved. And your sex life is nobody's business but your own. I respect your right to privacy."

Vanessa hardly heard him. "If my brothers knew . . ." Anxiously, she ran her fingers through her hair. "They all lost their virginity in high school, every one of them, even Ricky, who's five years younger than I am."

"I realize that you Ramseys are competitive, but there are certain areas in which one shouldn't feel the need to compete. Sex is one of them, Vanessa. I'm sure no one is keeping score."

"I've heard all the jokes about virgins and ingenues and good girls they've made over the years. I've even made them myself. I don't want anyone to find out that I *am* one!" She looked horrified at the possibility. "I'd never live it down."

"Your father would be inordinately relieved," Linc pointed out. "Celibacy is a sure way of avoiding—"

"Don't you dare suggest that I tell my father! At least he considers me enough of a woman to be sexually active. Knowing the truth would make me seem completely infantile in my parents' eyes." Her gray eyes narrowed and she fixed him with an unwavering stare. "In fact, there's only one way out of this impossible dilemma of mine. Since you're the only one who's ever guessed the truth about me, you should be the one to—"

"Deflower you?" Linc suggested dryly. "Initiate you into the pleasures of the flesh? Oh, baby, you don't know how much I'd like to oblige."

"All right," Vanessa said decisively, lying back on the bed. "Let's get to it."

"It's not that simple, Vanessa."

"Why not? You were certainly willing enough a short while ago when you thought I was a hot babe who knew all the tricks of the trade."

His lips curved into a ghost of a smile. "Vanessa, I

never thought of you as a hot babe who knew all the tricks of the trade. I did think you were sexually experienced and ready for a physical relationship with me. Now I see things differently. You're responsive and passionate but you're nervous and uncertain, too. I think we should wait until our wedding night to make love for the first time."

Vanessa felt a major tantrum welling up inside her. Bad enough that he should learn her guilty secret, but for him to brand her a nervous virgin who could only handle sex when safely married was a devastating blow to her carefully cultivated image of herself as a sophisticated bon vivant.

Her two sisters-in-law, Shavonne and Erin, flashed briefly to mind. She had always considered them the quintessential old-fashioned good girls, but even they had slept with their husbands prior to marriage. Her temper boiled. "I don't want to wait. Anyway, who says we're going to have a wedding night?"

"I do. And I—"

"I'm not going to let you turn me into the world's oldest living ingenue out of some stupid misguided sense of honor!" she exploded, sitting up and grasping his shoulders. "Now make love to me, dammit!"

She wrapped her arms around him and dragged him down on top of her. When she tried to capture his mouth with hers, he turned his head, evading her. She grabbed his face and held it between her hands. "Keep still!" she ordered.

"While you zero in for the kill? Er, excuse me, the kiss, that is."

"Linc, that's not fair!" she complained even as her lips quivered with laughter. The absurdity of the situation hadn't escaped her—she'd simply hoped she could ignore it. Unfortunately, it was time to face the truth, which wasn't at all funny. She sighed gloomily. "Don't think that I don't know what's wrong, Linc. I do. My virginity turned you off."

"Vanessa, that's not true. In fact, I want you more than ever."

"I don't believe you. If you really wanted me, you'd prove it."

He wondered how to deal with her tenacity. Lightly? He gave it a try. "This is a switch. Usually it's the guy who demands that the girl prove her feelings for him."

"I'm making a complete fool of myself, aren't I?" Vanessa felt as if she were going to cry. She wanted to sink with mortification.

He immediately regretted his attempt at humor. "I wasn't make fun of you, honey," he said softly. It seemed she could take anything but that. He wondered if her brothers knew how much pain their jocular, brotherly torment had caused her over the years. She didn't dare reveal sensitivity or doubt or fear because she fully expected to be mocked for it.

"Vanessa, I'm a possessive man, and I want you more than I've ever wanted any woman. The thought of being your first lover makes me feel—well, primitive—and fiercely protective and determined to be your *only* lover. If I make love to you now, you'll have to accept the fact that I'll never let you go. That I'm not merely relieving you of your unwanted virginity, but binding you to me forever."

She stared at him, heat searing every inch of her, her nerves aflame from the evocative effect of his words. Could she cope with such a commitment? Did she even want to? All her life she'd been fighting to keep her identity amid the smothering demands of her family. Had she unconsciously avoided serious emotional involvement because of it? And now here was Lincoln Scott making demands . . . and promises.

"What about that freedom you talked about?" she asked shakily.

"Sexual freedom? Never!" he said roughly. "But I wouldn't hold you back professionally and I'd encourage your independence. I want a whole, competent woman not a dependent little girl, Vanessa."

She stared at him, her gray eyes round and vulnerable. She'd always found it so easy to say no to a man, but now—

Lincoln Scott wasn't just any man. She ached when she looked at him. So this was what it was like to truly want, to profoundly need? She felt that if Linc were to leave her, she would lose a part of herself, perhaps the best part, a part that had yet to be revealed. She didn't want to risk that, she couldn't. "Stay with me, Linc," she said in a husky, thick voice that she hardly recognized as her own.

His dark blue eyes burned into hers. "Vanessa, I don't want there to be any misunderstandings. I've laid down my terms and by not objecting, you've tacitly agreed to them."

She didn't want to talk anymore, though she silently admitted that what he said was true. Verbalizing her acquiescence was another matter, however. She couldn't, not yet. But she could express her feelings in another way. With trembling fingers, she began to unfasten the buttons of his shirt. It seemed to take forever, but he didn't attempt to help her—or to stop her. He didn't take his eyes from her face as she slipped the shirt from his shoulders.

She stared at him in pure feminine fascination. His skin was tanned a light gold. Broad shoulders sloped down to the wide muscles of his chest which tapered to a flat stomach and narrow waist. She ran her fingers through the dark-blond mat of wiry-soft hair, loving the virile feel of him.

Perhaps they should wait until they were married to make love, Linc thought—she was a virgin, didn't she deserve his restraint?—but at this moment every bit of his restraint, resolve, and control were rapidly being erased by the seductive temptress who was staring at him with raptly admiring eyes and touching him with fingers of fire. He wanted her to want him with the same passionate intensity that he wanted her, he wanted to shred her virginal control and watch her come apart in his arms.

He lost himself in kissing her again and again,

kisses as deep and hot and wild as the sensations flaming within both of them.

"I want to see you, Vanessa," Linc said, skimming his hands over the smooth line of her dress. He fingered the top tiny buttons of her shirt, the rest of which disappeared inside the bodice of the dress.

Vanessa knew that it could have been awkward, undressing for the first time before a man, but Linc made it natural and easy for her. And when he gazed at her as if she were the most exquisite and appealing woman he'd ever seen, she felt as if she were exactly that.

With a soft sigh, she linked her arms around his neck and they kissed with slow, melting sensuality. His hands were so strong yet so gentle, so knowing. His mouth was hot and hard and hungry, drawing forth an equally fevered response from her.

How had she lived without this? Vanessa wondered achingly as the surging pleasure dissolved all her doubts and inhibitions. How had she lived without him?

His caresses, his kisses sensitized every inch of her skin. Every nerve ending burned with fiery need. When his mouth suckled her breast, she felt a burst of flame deep in her womb, a sharp, hot slash of pleasure so fierce it almost bordered on pain.

Dazed with passion, she was only vaguely aware of him shrugging out of his clothes but the sight of him, nude and aroused as he came to her, made her tremble. A volatile mixture of passion and tenderness, the force of which she had never before experienced, swept through her. She felt incredibly possessive of him as she ran her hands over him, learning the textures of his body.

"Vanessa!" he muttered as her soft hands swept over him. "Sweetheart, you're making me crazy."

A pleased little smile of feminine triumph curved her mouth. "Good," she said huskily, continuing her erotic explorations. She felt sensual and wild and free. "I want to make you crazy for me. I want to make you forget there ever was a Julia or a Karen or anyone else before me."

She was aware that her impulsive, impassioned declaration revealed the depth of her feelings for him. But she was given no time to ruminate, for Linc was gazing into her eyes, his own eyes glowing with intense blue flames. "It's never been like this with anyone, Vanessa." His fingers sought the hot, melting core of her and she gave a soft, sweet cry.

"You're mine," he said fiercely. "You'll never feel this way with anyone but me, you'll never want anyone but me."

There was unmistakable dominance in his possessive words, but Vanessa didn't rail against it. She understood his need to claim her as his; hadn't she done just that a moment earlier? It had nothing to do with supremacy and had everything to do with . . .

Her mind fogged and she lost her train of thought as Linc whispered something dark and sexy in her ear. His hand was deep between her legs, his fingers inside her, gliding through her flowing warmth, caressing her, learning her most intimate secrets. The feelings he was arousing in her were almost too exquisite, too delicious to endure. She clung to his strong, reassuring frame, moving helplessly against him as she whimpered with pleasure.

And yet, suddenly, it wasn't enough. She wanted more than physical ecstasy, however sublime. The burgeoning feelings she had for Linc, the voluptuous need. "Linc," she whispered through a haze of sensual bliss, "can't we be in love while we're making love? For just a little while?"

Eight

It was just the sort of thing a dewy-eyed, romantic young virgin would say, Vanessa berated herself later as she guided the boat through the unexpectedly choppy waters of the Gulf. She had to watch this tendency to blurt out her thoughts when she was around Linc, especially when her thoughts were as naive and emotional as *that*! Wanting to be in love to make love! Oh, Vanessa, you really are the world's oldest living ingenue, she scorned herself. She cast a covert glance at Linc. He was sitting beside her, close, but not touching, and he was watching her intently.

She blushed and though she willed herself not to, her perverse capillaries refused to obey. She was grateful for the dusky twilight which she hoped would conceal her embarrassingly girlish response.

"You're very pensive," Linc observed in his calm, matter-of-fact way, and just the sound of his voice made her quiver. She wanted to reach over and touch him. She wanted him to hold her, to kiss her and whisper outrageously sexy words to her in that low, husky growl his voice became when he was aroused.

Her pulses jumped and she felt a syrupy warmth suffuse her limbs. It took every ounce of willpower she possessed to keep her eyes open and on the water, every bit of concentration to keep her hands steady on the wheel. For memories of this afternoon were flowing over her in a sensual flood.

In her mind's eye, she saw and experienced it all over again. Linc's face, darkly intense, as he thrust into her feminine softness, which was so ready to receive him. She heard herself cry out his name and she heard his voice soothing and gentle and reassuring.

But it hadn't been a cry of pain or fear. From the moment her body had adjusted to his virile strength within her, she had loved it. She had reveled in the exquisite fullness of him deep inside her; she wanted it to go on and on. And when he had begun to move, she had been stunned by the intense, spiraling waves of pleasure which had pulsed and throbbed, gathering force within her.

She'd felt her senses spinning out of control as she locked herself convulsively around Linc. His breathing was as rapid and shallow as her own, his eyes glazed with a passion that matched hers, and it seemed to Vanessa that having Linc deep within her, a part of her, taking pleasure from her body and giving her pleasure with his, was everything she could ever want in the world.

And then the pounding force within her exploded, radiating shock waves of pure physical rapture which pulsed through her body in a cataclysmic burst of pleasure. She heard Linc call her name as he held her with shuddering strength, and she knew that she had pulled him into that sensuous maelstrom with her.

She remembered the languorous, drowsy aftermath, lying in his arms, her body warm and glowing and gloriously relaxed. They had talked a little and kissed a little and then her memory faded, for she had fallen into a deep, long sleep from which he had awakened her only a short while ago.

"Sweetheart, it's starting to get dark," Linc had said, gently rubbing her shoulder. "I think we'd better head back."

She'd stared at him, disoriented in the abrupt transition from deep sleep to wakefulness. "I don't want to get up," she'd murmured drowsily. "Let's stay here all night." She'd reached for him, wanting to cuddle and cling and forget the rest of the world and everyone else in it.

But Linc had been insistent. They couldn't possibly spend the night here, much as he'd like to, he had said. Her parents would be frantic with worry if they didn't turn up. Quentin Ramsey was likely to dispatch the Coast Guard to search for them.

His mention of her father's name chilled her, and an unwelcome, niggling doubt crept into her mind. Was he seeking to protect his credentials as the prime choice for her hand? Foolishly, she'd managed to forget just how and why they happened to be together today. But had Linc forgotten, for even a moment?

A slow flush heated her skin as she remembered his insistence on "protecting her," as he had so gentlemanly phrased it. The sight of the package of condoms had momentarily caught her off guard.

"Did you come prepared, hoping—or knowing—that you'd get me into bed today?" she'd asked, too lost in passion to really care but unable to resist asking the question.

Linc had given her a reassuring smile. "No, but apparently Jed had expectations for today. I found these in the drawer of the bedside table. Your father doesn't have to worry about him as much as he thinks."

And then he had murmured something private and sexy and wickedly funny, and their mutual laughter had been as warm and spontaneous and unifying as their loving.

What had happened to the open and passionate man who had been her afternoon lover? Vanessa wondered. Since awakening her, he had been relentlessly practical and logical, so . . . actuarial. She longed to slip beneath the barriers of his self-control and seduce him into casting common sense to the winds. She was willing to risk more than a Coast Guard hunt to make love with him again. But he'd left the cabin and she could hear him pulling up the anchor, so she'd reluctantly climbed out of bed.

And now they were speeding toward the marina and she felt unsure and uncertain and terrifyingly vulnerable. She'd never felt this way about any other man. The depth and strength of her feelings gave him an enormous power over her, one she'd never granted anyone else.

"Vanessa?" He stroked her cheek. "Honey, are you all right?"

No, Vanessa replied in her head, she was not all right. She needed to establish distance and regain her emotional equilibrium. She reminded herself that he didn't want to spend the night making love and pretending that there was anything more between them than sex—and that she did.

Her lips curved into a wry smile. One afternoon of passion had satisfied his need for her. Now he thought he could put her on ice while he kowtowed to her father. But the intensity of her feelings for him burned too hot for her to cool. Their passionate interlude had only intensified her need for him.

They were hopelessly at odds, Vanessa acknowledged grimly, and she was the one on the losing end. It was definitely time to regroup her defenses. "I'm fine," she said, struggling to sound blasé. "Why wouldn't I be?"

Linc stared at her. He could feel her withdrawing from him and he wondered why. Because she was having doubts and regrets about what had happened between them today? A flash of heat seared him as he remembered in vivid detail every moment of their lovemaking. He had wanted and needed her more desperately, more intensely than he had allowed himself to believe. He'd never known a woman could make him lose himself in the madness of passion, but Vanessa had done exactly that. He knew he was a technically competent lover who could satisfy a woman while taking his own pleasure, but what had occurred between Vanessa and him this afternoon had rendered every previous experience pallid and superficial.

Afterward, he had watched her sleep for a long time. She'd looked so sweet and vulnerable lying there, yet he couldn't forget how she had flamed like a torch in his arms. Her volatility and vulnerability was an irresistible combination evoking an equally paradoxical response in him. Every time he looked at her he wanted simultaneously to ravish her and to protect her. Which had made for a difficult afternoon. He'd wanted to awaken her countless times and make love to her again, but her own words, her wistful, whispered, *"Can't we be in love while we're making love? For just little while?"* stopped him every time. She'd been a virgin and he'd rushed her into a sexual relationship that she wasn't ready for because he couldn't keep his hands off her, he silently rebuked himself. It was uncharacteristic of him to act on impulse against his better judgment, but he'd done just that by taking Vanessa Ramsey to bed because he was aching for her, on fire for her.

He should have restrained himself, his calm rational self lectured his fiery alter ego. Never in his well-ordered life had he taken a woman he'd known only two days to bed, but when he touched Vanessa all the rules, all the shoulds seemed to evaporate. The spontaneous and passionate man who'd emerged was a side of himself he'd never realized existed. But Vanessa had inspired him and what they'd shared had been the most incredible, wonderful, mind-and-soul-shattering experience of his life.

Except now he felt guilty and selfish that he hadn't let her set the pace. He should have waited until their wedding night, he chided himself, for he knew with an unshakable certainty that they *would* have a wedding night. When it came to getting what he wanted he was implacable and determined; Quentin

Ramsey had been correct in that assessment of his character.

As Vanessa lay sleeping, Linc made a silent vow to her and to himself. From now on, there would be no more sexual pressure from him. If Vanessa needed to feel that she was in love with him before they made love again, then he would give her the time to fall in love with him.

He had no such need himself, Linc admitted, gazing at her exquisite profile as she concentrated on steering the boat. He knew he was already in love with her. And knowing that, it was impossible for him to spend the night with her on this boat without taking her, again and again. Oh, he knew he could make her want him. She was so responsive and passionate and he was her first lover, the man who had sexually awakened her. He knew exactly what to do to her, how to touch her, where to touch her . . .

His thoughts made his blood hot and his mind cloud. It was hard to remember his noble purpose: to give Vanessa the time to fall in love with him. Because sex wasn't enough for her. Nor for him, he reminded himself. The next time she had to be in love and not just for one afternoon.

During the trip back to the Ramsey house—with her driving the Aston Martin Volante this time, with the top up—he made several more conversational sallies, all of which she returned with a curt flippancy. He recognized the cool persona she was projecting, she was playing her role of society princess to the hilt. She was so different from the warm and loving woman he had taken to bed this afternoon. Impatience surged through him. Maybe he should take her back to bed, he mused. If that was where she could drop her guard and be herself, then why not start there?

He immediately chastised himself for the idea. It was entirely too self-serving. He had to be patient, to give her time. If that meant breaking through the wall of ice and sarcasm that she was building around herself all over again, that's what he would do.

Vanessa turned up the volume on the car radio and pretended to ignore Linc. She knew she was behaving badly, alternating cool silences with sardonic remarks and bored, condescending stares. She'd slipped effortlessly into the role of supercilious bitch that she'd been playing for years. But tonight it was a thin façade, and she knew it.

Tears burned behind her eyelids and her throat felt constricted by the boulder-sized lump in it. How far did she have to go to get a genuine response from him? No matter what she said, no matter how nastily she said it, Linc reacted with a kind of bland tolerance which spelled indifference to her. Why was he taking this from her? she wondered, seething with frustration. Surely he didn't like her this way? Unless . . .

She felt her heart sink. Unless he sought the distance which all the sparring and fencing created. Perhaps he preferred the sophisticated, caustic and cool Vanessa to the clinging, inexperienced innocent that he'd discovered in bed today?

It began to make sense in a weird, miserable way. He'd been willing to marry her for the opportunity to advance his career; such an arrangement didn't exactly call forth visions of true love. He hadn't expected to be saddled with an overemotional, lovesick virgin. *Which was the way she'd behaved in bed this afternoon.*

Her stomach churned with anxiety when she reminded herself that he hadn't wanted to stay with her tonight. Because he didn't want to have to go through a repeat performance?

She felt the color drain from her face and she went hot and cold at the same time as the truth struck her. She was a flop in bed! From time to time she'd heard her brothers laugh about women who were "lousy in bed" and she'd laughed along with them though she hadn't been exactly sure what that meant.

She still didn't, but she'd bet that being a pathetically eager and inexperienced virgin who tried to wring words of love from her lover definitely qualified for "lousy."

Rigid with pain, she swung the Volante into the long, wide drive leading to the Ramsey home. She'd learned long ago to block out hurt and convert her strongest emotions into anger. She handled anger well, she was magnificent when she was angry. But she seemed to have temporarily lost that power. She was too dejected and dispirited to summon even a semblance of wrath. She hurt too much, she cared too much.

"Vanessa."

Linc's voice jarred her. Her mouth felt dry and she didn't trust herself to speak.

"Vanessa," he repeated and cleared his throat. "Honey, I just want you to know that I've never had a day like this one with you."

She silently congratulated him on his choice of words. So smooth, so diplomatic. *"I've never had a day like this one with you."* She read her own meaning into it. "I'll just bet you haven't," she muttered darkly. She braked the car to a stop in front of the house and swiftly climbed out.

Linc caught her as she raced onto the porch. "Vanessa, talk to me. Tell me what's wrong."

"Why should anything be wrong? You've never had a day like this one before and neither have I. So that makes us even, doesn't it?"

"Are you ashamed of what we did, Vanessa?" he persisted. "Because you shouldn't be. Honey, we're going to be married and—"

A wave of pure rage surged through her at last. "I am *not* going to marry you, Lincoln Scott, not even if—"

The front door was flung open and Quentin Ramsey stood before them. "Vanessa, Lincoln!" His face was wreathed in smiles and he held out his arms as if to embrace them both. "I knew I'd heard a car out here. Come in, come in, we've all been waiting for you!"

"Waiting for us?" Vanessa echoed warily. "I thought you and the boys were in Idaho."

"We were, but we made it a point to be back early this evening. We'd never miss a night as important as this one. Did you have a good time on the boat today, kitten? I was starting to get concerned. If you'd stayed out much longer I'd've called the Coast Guard to look for you." Quentin laughed indulgently at his own paternal anxieties as he draped one arm around Vanessa's shoulder and the other around Linc's and propelled them inside.

A crowd seemed to burst forth from nowhere, filling the enormous entrance hall. Vanessa and Linc were swept up in it, hugged, kissed, and congratulated. All the Ramseys were there, Vanessa noted, with mounting apprehension—her parents, her brothers and their wives and children. Even Ricky had been summoned home from college. Shavonne and Erin's two youngest sisters, teen-aged Colleen and Megan Brady, were also present, although Tara Brady, the middle sister, was not.

She didn't know the other half of the crowd, but they knew Linc. They were hugging him and pounding him on the back, and she knew at once that they were his foster family, the Harrisons. She cast a sharp glance at her father, who was beaming with unabashed pleasure and didn't have to guess who was responsible for bringing Linc's family to Texas. Her apprehension turned to horror.

A plump, smiling woman caught Vanessa's hand and squeezed it. "I'm Linc's mother, Joy Harrison, Vanessa. It's so wonderful to meet you." Before Vanessa could react, the older woman gave her a swift hug. "And I'd like to welcome you to our family. You must be someone very special if our Linc loves you. I know the two of you will be very happy together."

"Thank you, Joy." Quentin Ramsey stepped in,

accepting the compliments and congratulations as his due. "We feel exactly the same way."

"Lincoln, dear, why don't you introduce Vanessa to the rest of the family?" Joy suggested, beaming from Quentin to Vanessa to Linc.

Vanessa was shoved back to Linc's side. She was too stunned to speak, but no one seemed to notice or to expect her to do anything but stand beside Linc as he introduced her to an inordinate number of relatives. His grandmother, his aunt, his brothers, their wives, his sister, her husband, and a slew of nieces and nephews, Vanessa met them all. Their names swirled around her head, lost in a din of noise and confusion. Bob, Jean, Timmy, Christy, Joycie, Ken, Kenny, Lori, Rob, Diane, Randy, and Angela. There were others; she knew she'd never remember them or keep them all straight.

They were all here to celebrate her engagement to Lincoln, that much was obvious. A huge silk banner proclaiming CONGRATULATIONS was hung across the string of Japanese lanterns in the garden, long covered tables were loaded with food and fresh flowers, a bar had been set up around the pool while Jed played bartender to the crowd.

Someone—Joy Harrison?—handed Vanessa a plate piled high with food and urged her to sit down and eat because a bride-to-be needed to keep up her strength for the wedding festivities.

Vanessa debated if she should scream or faint and ended up doing neither. She seemed to be in a state of shock. She stood with the heaping plate in her hand, staring dazedly at the crowd. Her father was playing the genial host, treating the adult Harrisons to whopping doses of his forceful charm, and her mother and Joy Harrison were actually giggling together like a pair of giddy schoolgirls. The mob of Harrison children chased each other through the gardens and around the pool, pausing now and then to snatch food from the buffet tables. Linc was being monopolized by his elderly grandmother and aunt and he appeared to be listening to them attentively.

It probably wouldn't be a wise move to dump her plate of food over his head, Vanessa decided, although she was sorely tempted. Not while he was standing with those two sweet-faced little old ladies who were gazing at him as if he were the Messiah.

"This was certainly unexpected."

She turned at the sound of her brother Rad's voice. He was holding two glasses of champagne and handed one to her. "To say the least!" she said numbly.

"I take it you had no idea that Dad had imported the Harrisons for this party tonight?"

Vanessa shook her head mutely.

"I thought not. The look on your face when you arrived said it all." Rad took a sip of his drink. "Dad's ensconced the entire Harrison clan—all nineteen of them—in the Park Mall Hotel for the week."

Vanessa gasped. "They'll be here for a whole week?"

"Sure. It wouldn't make much sense for them to go back to Kansas, only to return for the wedding on Saturday."

The glass of champagne and the plate stacked with food slipped from her hands and hit the stone terrace. Crystal and china weren't noted for their longevity in a Ramsey home. *The wedding?*

Three young Harrisons tromped obliviously through the pile of spilled food. Rad took Vanessa's arm and guided her out of the way. "Vanessa, what's going on?" he demanded. "You're acting as if you know nothing about your own wedding." He paused, then raised his brows, comprehension dawning in his gray eyes. "It was supposed to be a secret, wasn't it? Just as you've kept this Lincoln Scott a secret from the family. You wanted to avoid a big society splash and elope and the folks found out and rearranged things their way."

Vanessa longed to tell him the truth. At this moment, she wanted her brother's help and advice more than anything, but she had no idea how to ask for it. Their family dynamics didn't operate that way—Ramseys kept their own counsel and announced only their triumphs, never their weaknesses, uncertainties, or failures. She was able to talk to Rad about her frustrations in the office, but this . . . this was so personal. And so utterly humiliating! If she were to tell Rad that their father had bribed Lincoln Scott to marry her because he was sexually safe in this era of sexual danger, Rad would certainly tell his wife. He told her everything. And then Erin would tell her sisters—how could she resist passing along such a choice morsel of gossip?

And Vanessa well knew how quickly gossip spread. Jed would find out. So would Melinda Sue Harper and Lexie Madison. Her face burned. She couldn't bear it. At least she had a modicum of public pride now; if that story ever got around, even that would be lost. That bit of pride was all she had left and she clung to it with Ramsey-like tenacity.

She looked her oldest brother in the eye and shrugged. "You have a mind like the proverbial steel trap, Rad. No wonder you're president of the company."

"Well, take heart," Rad said encouragingly. "Not even Dad and Mother were able to pull off a great white extravaganza in such a short time. The wedding is to be small and private with only the two families in attendance." He gazed around at the noisy, merry crowd. "Although I suppose it's a bit of a contradiction in terms to call any event involving this mob small and private," he added dryly.

He leaned down and unexpectedly kissed her cheek. "I'm happy for you, Vanessa. The folks think the world of your Lincoln Scott, and you know how choosy they are when it comes to the right man for their little princess. He must be a great guy. I'm looking forward to getting to know him."

Vanessa felt tears well in her eyes. She didn't expect sentimental, brotherly gestures from any of her brothers; they'd certainly never indulged in them before. But Rad had changed so much since he'd married Erin. She knew he was happier than he'd ever been. Touched, she put her arms around his neck and gave him a quick, awkward hug.

Linc chose that moment to join them. Rad introduced himself and heartily shook his hand. Vanessa jerked into rigidly erect, military-like posture. "Having a good time, Lincoln?" she asked through clenched teeth, her gray eyes glinting with fury.

"Wonderful. It's been quite some time since I've seen my family," Linc returned pleasantly, meeting and holding her gaze.

"Thanks to my father, you get to spend the entire week with them." She tried to smile, for Rad's benefit, but she suspected she looked more like a she-wolf baring its fangs. "Culminating with *our wedding* on Saturday."

"Uh-oh," said Rad. "Vanessa isn't happy that Dad interfered with your plans to elope. And I've learned that it isn't much fun—or very safe—to be around when Vanessa isn't happy." He gave Linc a sympathetic clap on the back. "I think I'll leave you two to thrash this out between you."

"What plans to elope?" Linc asked interestedly as Rad made a quick getaway.

"I let him think that because it was easier than trying to explain what a devious, manipulative, sociopathic cad you are!" she spat at him. "You knew all about this party tonight! You conspired with my father to keep me out on the boat all day. That's why you were so insistent that we come back here tonight—because you knew your whole family and mine were going to be here celebrating our engagement!"

And then the full impact of her accusation struck her. If the reason Linc didn't want to spend the night on the boat was because he knew about the party and had to get her back to the house that meant . . . That meant he hadn't insisted on leaving because he didn't want to spend the night with her!

That meant he didn't think she was lousy in bed and wanted to avoid making love with her?

She felt suddenly weak with relief. It was insane, but she was glad! Glad that there was another reason for his insistence on leaving the boat than the dreadful one she'd feared. Which meant she was glad that he'd conspired with her father to trap her into this pretense of an engagement in front of both their families? Oh, she was insane, all right, Vanessa thought grimly. Or maybe she was in love. Weren't the two said to be somewhat synonymous?

She glanced up at him and her heart turned over. Oh damn, she *was* in love with him! She didn't know how or why it had happened so fast but she knew it was irrevocable. And she knew that he didn't love her. Linc was attracted to her physically and monetarily. But he wasn't in love with her.

"How did I ever get into this fix?" she snapped at him. She was enraged. No man backed Vanessa Ramsey into a corner, no man took control of her and maneuvered her into anything. No man had ever dared to make her fall in love with him, either. Except Lincoln Scott.

Lincoln Scott, the exception to every rule about her, stood before her and shrugged casually. "I don't suppose you'd believe that I knew absolutely nothing about this party or my family's arrival in Houston or our alleged wedding on Saturday?"

"You're damn right I wouldn't believe it!"

"I didn't think so. Why would you take the word of a devious, manipulative, sociopathic cad?"

His dry humor, his droll expression almost made her giggle. But then Linc reached over to tuck a loose strand of her hair behind her ear and she went weak and trembly from just that slight touch. She wanted nothing more than to be alone with him, to laugh with him about their impossible relatives, to touch his face and run her hands over his muscular frame, to kiss him . . . Oh, he had her hooked, all right! Vanessa acknowledged grimly. She got mad at him all over again.

"I demand that you tell everyone that this is strictly a farce. That there is no engagement and there isn't going to be any wedding." She gave him a push. "Go on, make an announcement. Now!"

"Not me, honey," Linc drawled. "As far as I'm concerned we are engaged. And we are going to be married. I've told you that right from the start. So if there is any announcement to the contrary, you'll have to be the one to make it."

Vanessa stared around at the cheerful, festive throng. Everyone seemed so happy. She'd never seen her mother smile so much, not even when her brothers got married. There was a certain, special cachet in being Mother of the Bride, she'd once heard her mother remark. From what she could see, Nola Ramsey was thoroughly caught up in it. And then there was her maddening, controlling, overprotective, but everloving father. Though there had been times in her life when she had willed Quentin Ramsey to disappear into a big, black hole he had also found Linc for her.

Vanessa swallowed as her gaze fastened compulsively on Linc, her first lover, the only lover she ever wanted. She was in love with him and that was the crux of her dilemma. But she wasn't about to admit it to him, not when he hadn't said a word about loving her. The Ramsey pride could not tolerate a confession of unrequited love.

"I'm not going to be the one to ruin everyone's good time," she said crossly, knowing how weak an excuse that was. There had been countless times in the past when she'd ruined everyone's good time without a second thought.

"Then I guess we're still engaged." Linc took her hand and lifted it to his mouth. His tongue traced small circles along her sensitive palm in a private and erotic gesture that made her shudder with a spasm of delight. "When do you want to go shopping for a ring?"

She jerked her hand back. There was a heavy throb rippling through her abdomen. Her nipples were already taut and sensitive beneath the soft cotton of her dress. Her gaze flew to his mouth and she trembled. And rebelled against the urgent desire to surrender to him, then and there. "When hell freezes over!" she said instead.

"I left myself wide open for that one," Linc observed calmly, reaching into the pocket of his shirt. He pulled out a small black book with a short pen attached to it.

"You've had that thing with you all day?" She watched, wide-eyed and incredulous, as he flipped through the pages.

"I'm never without it."

"I thought you said you didn't have a little black book filled with the names of your conquests," she reminded him tautly.

"Relax, Vanessa, this is my appointment book. I'm an actuary, remember. We're very precise, very scheduled. We live by our appointment books. Now, how about Monday? We'll go to lunch and then to the jewelry store."

She watched him write in the little book, then snatched it from him and leafed through it. "Enrolled Actuaries Meeting. Lunch with Jack W. Lunch with Steve R. Quarterly office staff meeting. ASPA conference in Dallas," she read aloud. "What's that?"

"The American Society of Pension Actuaries," Linc said patiently.

"Sounds like a real hoot." She handed the book back to him, thrilled that it hadn't been filled with women's names and a schedule of his dates with them. "You lead the dullest life imaginable. What are you going to write down for Saturday? Marry Vanessa R.?"

His eyes gleamed. "The way things are going I'd better *pencil* that one in."

She silently acknowledged that their verbal joust was indicative of the sexual tension vibrating between them. It was exciting, exhilarating. "It's not going to happen, you know," she said archly, her eyes gleaming with feminine challenge. "There isn't going to be a wedding, no matter what everybody here thinks."

"Mmm."

Her ever-volatile temper flared. "You shouldn't be so sure of me!"

"But I am," he said affably. "You'll marry me because there'll be no more lovemaking until after the wedding."

"Oh!" Vanessa was incensed. "Your ego is so massive it's beyond the realm of comprehension! Do you actually think that I *want* any more of your lovemaking?"

He nodded, unruffled by her ire. "Yes, Vanessa. I actually think that."

She put her hands on her hips and glowered at him. "We're not just talking massive ego here, we're talking Olympian ego! Furthermore, what gives you the right to decide when and if we'll make love? I believe I have a say in the matter, too. I refuse to be subject to the will of another controlling male. Lord knows I've had more than my share with my father and my bro—"

"While we're on the subject of controlling males, let's turn to controlling females. You. I think you're deliberately trying to goad me into shutting you up," Linc interrupted, grinning with pure male challenge.

To which she reacted at once. "That's exactly the sort of chauvinistic remark I'd expect an atavistic type like you to make!"

"You do have a way with words." He pulled her into his arms with a husky laugh.

She turned her head to ward him off. "Let me go, Linc. I don't want this, ..." Her voice trailed off as she watched his head descend toward her, his blue eyes mesmerizing her with the intensity she saw in them. She trembled, her body already soft and pliant in his arms. Her mind spun away.

He captured her mouth in a long, lingering kiss. Her response was immediate and ardent, as if she'd been sensually conditioned. Perhaps she had at that. She was dazed and clingy when he finally released her. "Now tell me that you don't want me, Vanessa," he said, his voice a soft, seductive purr.

She bridled at his unconcealed masculine confidence. It would be so easy to tell him that she wanted him, that she loved him and was going to marry him, in spite of all the encouragement and enthusiasm from both families. But what Ramsey courtship ever went easily and smoothly? Not Rad's, not Slade's, and not their little sister Vanessa's. If there was a convoluted, complicated route to love and romance, the Ramseys unerringly followed it.

She gazed up at him with limpid gray eyes, her lips parted and softly swollen, her arms linked around his neck. "I want you, Lincoln," she whispered, slowly, sinuously rubbing her breasts against his chest.

His body jerked convulsively and he gripped her closer, harder, his arousal thick and virile and obvious. Vanessa smiled a siren's smile. "And you want me, too," she murmured, standing on tiptoe to take a sensuous bite of his ear lobe. She felt the forceful tremor shudder through him and thrilled to her own power over him.

"It's time you learned that you aren't calling all the shots, lover," she said in a husky, sexy voice totally at odds with the challenge she had issued. "I want you to take me home with you tonight."

Her proximity was having an addling effect on his willpower. His nostrils filled with her enticing scent, and he was flooded with a host of sensual memories. Of this afternoon when they had lain together, when he had thrust himself deep inside her, had become one with her.

He buried his face in the soft hollow of her neck and drew in a sharp breath. He was madly in love with her, but he'd vowed not to make love to her again until they were married, he recalled foggily. "No, Vanessa," he mumbled.

She heard the unsteadiness in his voice and laughter bubbled up within her. How could she have thought, even for a few misguided moments, that he no longer desired her? She was elated with his blatant proof of it. "No?" she teased, playfully running her hands over the taut curve of his buttocks. "Really, Lincoln? No?"

He tried to catch her hands. And failed. He groaned. "Vanessa, we—shouldn't."

She stroked the nape of his neck and moved against him in slow, sensual rhythm, feeling drunk on his devastating masculinity, adrift on pure sensation. Yet fighting for control. "But you will," she whispered, nuzzling his throat. "Won't you, Linc?"

His body was aching. She brushed her lips against his mouth and he felt as if the top of his head had come off. "Yes," he said thickly. "Oh, baby, let's go now. We can skip out on the rest of the party—everyone is having such a great time, I don't think they'll even notice we're gone."

She was tempted to do it. She wanted to go home with him and spend the night with him, talking and making love and finally falling asleep in his arms, in his bed. But before she could tell him so, she happened to glance over his shoulder and see her father approaching them, his expression triumphant as he spied his daughter in Lincoln Scott's arms.

They were in league against her, Vanessa reminded herself sternly. There was a power struggle going on and though she might ultimately lose the war, she was damn sure going to win some of the battles. This one. A Ramsey didn't go down without a fight. She pulled out of Linc's arms and shot him a gloating, gleeful smile. "So there'll be no more lovemaking until we're married, hmm?"

His eyes widened and he gaped at her.

"Poor Linc," she said mockingly. "You thought

you had me wrapped around your little finger, didn't you? You thought you had only to snap and I'd jump to your command. Well, think again, mister."

Linc ran a hand through his hair, wondering whether to laugh or to swear. He felt like doing both, simultaneously. "You set me up, didn't you, Vanessa?"

"All the way," she said breezily, not bothering to add that she'd almost been snared in her own trap along with him.

"You must be very pleased with yourself, Miss Ramsey. You're probably thinking that you have *me* wrapped around *your* little finger. That all you have to do is to crook that sweet little finger and I'll follow you anywhere."

Vanessa shrugged blithely. "Something like that. Care to dispute it?"

Before he could answer Quentin Ramsey swooped down on them and inserted himself between them. "Ah, here's the happy couple! One thing you're going to learn about the Ramseys, Linc, my boy, is that we're a very photographically inclined family. We have a photographer present for every important family event and tonight is certainly a milestone—the engagement party of our little girl. Now, come along, we need you two to pose for some very important pictures."

"Don't forget to smile, Lincoln," Vanessa said sweetly, flushed with her victory.

"I won't. But don't you forget that the last laugh is the best laugh."

"Which I'll have, come Saturday."

Quentin Ramsey beamed at his daughter. "Saturday. Your wedding day. You see, kitten, didn't Daddy tell you that everything would work out all right?"

Linc cleared his throat. Vanessa shot him a quick glance and saw his lips twitching with laughter. She watched her father smile at Linc, saw Linc return that smile. They thought they had it all worked out between them. She seethed. Daddy's little kitten was supposed to docilely accept the plan they'd mapped out for her and become Lincoln's little kitten. Worst of all, she was almost tempted to do just that.

Her gray eyes narrowed into slits. No, she decided. She'd had enough of playing the role assigned to her. It was time to write her own script. She smiled. She wasn't a princess or a pet, she was a woman. She intended to convince the men in her life of that fact, no matter what it took.

Nine

The Harrison clan planned to spend their first full day in Houston at Astroworld, the Texas-size amusement park across the street from the Astrodome, the world's first indoor, air-conditioned stadium. Quentin and Nola Ramsey insisted that Vanessa go with them. Vanessa flatly refused.

Linc hadn't even bothered to mention it to her, he simply arrived at the house the next morning expecting her to go along. Vanessa stayed in her room, fuming. Her parents came up to tell her that she absolutely *had* to go to Astroworld with the Harrisons and her fiancé. Vanessa told them that she had no intention of going. They departed after offering bribes, cajolery, and subtle threats, all of which Vanessa ignored.

She was wrapped in a short lavender silk robe applying a coat of berry-red nail polish to her fingernails when her brothers Jed and Ricky entered her bedroom. Without bothering to knock, of course.

"What are you up to now, Vanessa?" Ricky demanded.

She continued to polish her nails. "I don't know what you mean, sweetie."

"Daddy and Mama are freaking out because you won't go to Astroworld with Linc and his family." Her younger brother scowled at her. "Why won't you?"

She shrugged. "I hate Astroworld, you know that. I always have. I get motion sick on all the rides."

"Yeah, but you don't have to go on the rides. Just go along to the park and hang out with Linc. You're engaged to him, Vanessa," Ricky pointed out. "The poor guy," he added, his pale gray eyes glinting with kid-brotherly humor. "What kind of crime did he commit in his last life to get saddled with a karma like that?" He chuckled, pleased at his own wit.

Vanessa ignored him.

"Trouble in paradise already, Vanessa?" Jed fixed her with a penetrating stare. "Do you know what I think?" he proceeded to answer his own question. "I think there's something mighty fishy about this whole engagement. I thought so the moment you told me about it. But after hearing what I heard this morning, I *know* something's up. I don't think you want to marry this guy, this Lincoln Scott, at all, Vanessa. I think the folks are forcing you into it."

Ricky and Vanessa both stared at him. "It's true, isn't it?" Jed persisted. "And I've figured out why."

Vanessa jerked and smeared the polish on her thumbnail. "What are you talking about, Jed?"

"Vanessa, for heaven's sake, stop playing the heroine and let me help you!" he exclaimed in a concerned tone she had never heard him use before. "I know what's going on! Scott's got something on Dad and is blackmailing him. Marrying you is part of his payoff. Along with the pension contract and the indigo Maserati Quattroporte and the shares of stock in the company."

"An indigo Maserati Quattroporte? Wow!" Ricky gasped. "Where?"

"Dad just presented Lincoln Scott with the keys," Jed said tersely. "I was eavesdropping on the two of them in the den a few minutes ago. I heard Dad go down the entire list of what he was signing over to Scott on the day of the wedding."

"Cool!" Ricky enthused. "You can leave the church in his new car, Vanessa."

"Forget the car, you idiot," snapped Jed. "Didn't you hear what I just said? Vanessa's future is being sold in an extortion plot."

Vanessa stared at him strangely. "You heard Daddy tell Linc he was giving him those things?"

Jed caught her by the shoulders. "Vanessa, you can't go through with it! I won't let you! We'll work something out. You can't sacrifice your life this way!"

Why, he was serious, Vanessa marveled. He believed she was in trouble and was genuinely concerned. After all these years, to learn that her brother cared about her, that he loved her . . . she was enthralled. And she was almost tempted to play along with his theory, just to see what he would say and do next. But the realization that he cared was enough, she decided. She was tired of tricks and schemes and games of one-upmanship.

"Jed, Linc isn't blackmailing Daddy. And I'm not sacrificing myself. Honestly."

But Jed was not to be thwarted. "Yeah, yeah, tell me you want to marry an actuary, an ex-farmboy from Kansas. A guy with no cash, no flash. A guy who drives a *Pacer*, for crying out loud! Give it up, Vanessa. I know you. Lincoln Scott is nothing like the guys you've always dated and you expect me to believe that you're planning on marrying him? Admit it! If Dad weren't involved, you wouldn't have passed him a potato chip at a party."

Her face softened. "It's all very simple, Jed. The men I used to date were strictly for dating. Linc is for marrying. And since you know me, you know darn well that nobody could force me into marrying anyone against my will."

"You're not being forced, you're doing it of your own free will to save Dad's skin." Jed appeared genuinely disturbed by the notion. "Vanessa, you've got to trust me with this. Let me help you!"

What now? thought Vanessa. It was lovely knowing that Jed would help her when he feared she was to be the family sacrifice, but if she weren't, if he were to learn that her father was bribing Linc to marry her, rather than the other way around . . . She was still too wary of her brother's sharp tongue and caustic wit to impart that bit of information.

"Let me handle the situation in my own way, Jed," she told him. "I know what I'm doing." One of her bigger whoppers, she acknowledged. She'd never been more confused, befuddled, or ambivalent in her entire life.

Which Jed picked up on, of course. "Vanessa, I'm not going to allow Dad to throw you to the wolves—uh—wolf," Jed said impassionately. "I'm going to dig into this crime, I promise."

"Jed, don't!" she cried on a note of panic.

Quentin Ramsey joined them at that moment, accompanied by Linc. "Jed, stop upsetting your little sister," their father ordered sternly. Vanessa knew that his tendency to automatically blame her brother and take her part always infuriated Jed, but this time he didn't take offense. Instead, he touched Vanessa's arm and said fiercely, "I mean it, kid. You're no longer in this alone."

"Good morning, Vanessa," Linc said softly, his eyes on her, seemingly oblivious to the smoldering glares he was receiving from Jed and Ricky. He crossed the room and took her in his arms, leaning down to kiss her cheek lightly.

She reflexively relaxed against the hard strength of his body. He was wearing a yellow knit shirt and a well-worn pair of tight-fitting jeans which drew her attention to all of his masculine attributes. He looked wonderful and he felt wonderful, too. His big hands moved on her waist and she felt a pulsing, burning sensation in her lower body that was wildly exciting. The others seemed to fade from view, leaving her alone with Linc in a private moment all their own.

"Linc's here to take you to Astroworld, princess," Quentin's booming voice ended that brief, sweet intimacy. "Better hurry and get dressed."

"Oh, she's not coming with us," Linc put in swiftly. He smiled down at her. "Vanessa hates amusement parks, that's why I didn't even bother to ask her to join us. I just dropped by this morning to ask her to have dinner with me tonight."

Vanessa stared at him, disconcerted. "How do you know I hate amusement parks?" she asked.

"You told me so yesterday on the boat, remember? You said you always got motion sick on the rides."

Vanessa nodded slowly. They had talked for a long, long time on the boat, but her mention of amusement park rides had been merely a throwaway line, something she'd never expected him to remember. But he had. She was incredulous. And touched. Years of superficial conversation had led her to believe that no one listened to what anyone said, let alone remembered it. Damaging gossip excepted, of course.

She stared up at Linc with wide gray eyes. He listened to her, he remembered what she said and acted upon it. A sweet liquid heat suffused her. Suddenly, it didn't seem as important to take an unbending, adamant stand. "I suppose I could go to the park and stay off the rides," she said slowly. "You know, just walk around with you and your family."

"That wouldn't be any fun for you, honey. Have dinner with me tonight instead," replied Linc.

Vanessa frowned. She didn't want to wait until tonight to see him again, she wanted to spend the day with him. Anywhere, she realized with astonishment. Even in an amusement park. There had never been anybody whom she'd wanted to be with regardless of surroundings. So this was what it was like to be in love? she mused. And smiled suddenly.

"I'm coming with you," she said decisively. "Everybody, out of my room. I have to get dressed." She herded the four males out.

They paused in the hall, outside her closed door. "How did you do it?" Ricky asked, staring at Linc with awe. "How did you turn her around like that? She said she wasn't going to Astroworld, and once Vanessa makes up her mind, nobody can make her change it. But you did," he added admiringly.

"Yeah, he did." Jed's tone was not admiring. He

glared from his father to Linc. "But here's a word of warning, Scott. Don't start counting your stock certificates yet. Come on, Rick, we've got work to do." He caught his younger brother's arm and strode down the hall, dragging the boy after him.

"Don't pay any mind to Jed, Linc," advised Quentin, frowning after his son. "He's unhappy, out of sorts. As soon as you and Vanessa are married, I'll turn my energy to straightening out his life."

"I'm sure he'll be deeply appreciative of your efforts," Linc said dryly.

Vanessa emerged a few minutes later in a figure-hugging strapless coral sundress with shiny silver snaps from the top of the bodice to the bottom of the full skirt. She grinned at Linc's expression. The dress was eye-popping and she knew it. And though it wasn't in the least apropos for a day at the amusement park, she didn't care. Linc's reaction to the sight of it was her sole interest.

"All I have to do is to pull open those snaps and you'd be out of that dress," he remarked in a rather strangled whisper as they walked from the house to the shiny indigo Maserati Quattroporte parked in front.

"That's all," Vanessa agreed airily. "I like your new car. Jed told me about it."

"The car is yours, Vanessa," said Linc, his eyes studying the snaps. "I'm transferring the title to your name tomorrow."

"Don't. I don't want a Maserati, not even a Quattroporte. I plan to get a Bitter SC convertible."

Linc was floored by her offhand remark. "I've never even seen a Bitter SC except in exotic car magazines. And I can't accept a car from your father, Vanessa."

"You didn't seem to have any difficulty accepting the offer to design a pension plan for Ramsey & Sons," she reminded him.

"That's different. Services rendered for a standard fee."

"Daddy obviously considers the car in the same light." She glanced at him slyly. "The service is marrying me, of course. Some might say you deserve more than a fancy sports car for that daring deed."

Linc smiled slightly, then was serious once more. "Another thing, Vanessa. Your father offered me a sheaf of stock certificates which I also intend to have transferred to your name."

She looked bored. "Don't bother. I already have more stock than I know what to do with." She climbed into the passenger side of the Maserati Quattroporte.

"You're very spoiled, little girl." Linc slipped behind the wheel. Impulsively, he reached over and unsnapped the bottom snap of her skirt. She watched him without comment. He quickly unsnapped four more, opening the skirt to her knees.

"I'm not a little girl, Lincoln."

He swallowed. "No, Vanessa, you're not."

She crossed her legs and watched him stare at the long, shapely length of them. And smiled to herself. "Shall we go?"

"Oh! Uh, yes. Yes. I told the family I'd meet them at the main gate of the park at eleven o'clock. Your father chartered a bus to take all nineteen of them from the hotel to the park. Everyone was overwhelmed, to say the least."

"Oh, we Ramseys are overwhelming," Vanessa agreed pleasantly, "to say the least." She leaned back in the seat and closed her eyes. The action thrust her breasts forward and Linc couldn't tear his eyes away from the creamy soft swelling above the strapless bodice.

They didn't spend much time at Astroworld. The Harrison family—from the youngest toddler to seventy-eight-year-old Grandma—were having the time of their lives riding the rides, playing the games, and sampling a spectacular assortment of junk food. When Linc mentioned to his foster mother that everyone appeared to be having a great time and perhaps he and Vanessa were superfluous to the day's activities, Joy Harrison was quick to agree.

"You two run along," she said cheerfully, beaming at the couple. "We never expected you to spend the day with us, we know you'd rather be alone." She winked at Vanessa. "I haven't forgotten what it's like to be young and in love."

To her consternation, Vanessa blushed. Joy Harrison laughed in delight. "Off with you, now. Find a nice, private restaurant and have a cozy little lunch."

Linc fully intended to do just that. Then Vanessa asked him where he lived. He told her about his three-room apartment in an apartment complex several miles outside the Loop. She was unfamiliar with the neighborhood, and he decided it was easier to show her where it was than to try to describe its geographic position.

The moment they were standing in his small L-shaped living/dining room, filled with an eclectic assortment of secondhand furniture, he pulled her into his arms. "So much for finding a nice, private restaurant and having a cozy little lunch," he said, nuzzling her neck.

"I thought you brought me here for lunch," replied Vanessa, feigning a wide-eyed innocence. "Why else would we have come, since you don't intend to make love to me until after the wedding?"

Linc sat down on the sofa and pulled her onto his lap. "Are you going to throw that in my face all week?"

"Of course." She wriggled sensuously in his lap and boldly pulled his shirt from under his belt. A delicious little shiver coursed through her when she touched her hands to the hair-roughened bareness of his stomach.

Linc's breath caught in his throat. "Not so fast, honey. I'm already about to explode and I haven't even kissed you yet."

"Then we'd better get started," she whispered, lifting her mouth to his. He took it in an achingly tender kiss. Which swiftly deepened into fiery passion. Vanessa heard each snap of her dress pop open and shuddered with desire as she felt his big, warm hands move along the skin which he was baring. She wore only pale peach panties under her dress and he quickly dispensed with them along with the dress.

She trembled as he stroked her body, his fingers deft and insistent and sure. When he picked her up in his arms and carried her into his bedroom, she sighed, savoring the romantic gesture. He laid her on the bed and then lay down beside her, exploring all the soft curves of her body with his lips and his hands, caressing, arousing, making her thrill to his mastery.

"Oh, Linc," she whispered achingly, gazing into his eyes. She loved him. It was magic to be with him like this, just the two of them, close and intimate, touching and kissing and loving.

"My sweet, hot little lover," he said possessively. "This is so good, so right. We belong together, Vanessa. For now, for always."

He took her completely, moving in a slow, arousing rhythm deeply within her until she was writhing beneath him with pleasure, crying his name aloud. They moved together, harder and faster, and Vanessa moaned and clung to him as a savage ripple of sheer ecstasy surged through her.

Linc rasped her name, his face a dark mask of passion. He felt her body convulse in a spasm of sweet shudders and held her to him, his expression exultant. And then he was carried away on the same tempestuous tide of passion.

She lay in his arms, sated and languid with fulfillment, a delicious lethargy sweeping through her. Linc held her, his hands stroking her gently with a tenderness that made her feel cherished and protected. She could hardly hold her eyelids open and they finally fluttered shut.

Linc kissed her forehead, her cheeks and her mouth lightly, lovingly. "Just like yesterday," he said softly. "You get very sleepy after climaxing. You need to take a nap."

Her eyes flew open and she stirred in his arms. The intimate observation made her blush. "Go to sleep, sweetheart," Linc said softly. "I'll stay with you. I'll hold you. Close your eyes."

Vanessa felt supremely, sublimely content. She never wanted him to let her go. She wanted to tell him that she had fallen in love with him, that she wanted to make him happy, not just sexually, but in every way. But she was so drowsy, and his soft words and caresses were lulling her into sleep. The words drifted in her mind as her thoughts faded into sweet oblivion.

Linc arrived at his office shortly before ten on Monday morning, the first time he'd ever come so late to work in his life. He wondered what Ben, his actuarial assistant, and Joan, the secretary-receptionist, would think of his lapse from punctuality. They were accustomed to him being precise and predictable, the actuary's actuary, as Joan had dubbed him, not altogether in jest, Linc suspected.

He'd slept through his alarm this morning, another unheard-of occurrence in his scheduled, well-ordered life. But he'd had a very late night last night. He hadn't taken Vanessa home until well after midnight, and after a long and tender parting kiss, he'd been cornered by Quentin who proceeded to give a jovial, blow-by-blow account of the barbecue which he and Nola had thrown that evening for the Harrisons. Nobody seemed to mind that Linc and Vanessa had missed it. The old adage "everybody loves a lover" seemed entirely true as far as the Ramseys and the Harrisons were concerned.

With one exception. Jed Ramsey. He had been waiting for Linc outside, inspecting the dashing Maserati Quattroporte with a fierce scowl. He had also drunk one too many margaritas at the barbecue and wasn't making much sense as he made innuendoes and vague, dark references to . . . blackmail? Linc had puzzled over Jed's rantings, but none of it made much sense. One thing was obvious, however, Jed Ramsey wasn't looking forward to becoming his brother-in-law.

Linc spent a good part of his drive to work this morning wondering why. Did Vanessa's brother dislike him personally? Or did he disapprove of the haste with which the wedding date had been set? A sudden thought struck him, and a flush warmed his skin. Suppose Jed believed the reason for such urgency was an unplanned pregnancy? That would certainly explain his hostility. It would be damn hard for an older brother to gladhand the man he believed had made his little sister pregnant out of wedlock.

Vanessa. Pregnant with his child. For a moment Linc allowed himself to entertain the idea. She was the one woman in the world whom he wanted to bear his child, he thought, his blood heating with pleasure. Someday . . .

He was still caught up in his daydream when Vanessa joined him in the tiny atrium of his small office complex. He blinked. She was dressed for success in a charcoal gray pin-stripe suit, a pale pink silk blouse betraying a glimpse of feminine softness. Her hair was pulled back into a professional chignon style and her black pumps were alarmingly sensible.

Linc stared at her in astonishment. He knew he had Vanessa Ramsey on the brain, but was this chairman-of-the-board image of her the hallucination of a tired mind?

"It's about time you showed up," Vanessa said briskly. "I've been here since quarter to eight."

Linc reached out to touch her and his fingers brushed the lightweight tropical worsted wool of her suit jacket. A whiff of her exotic and sexy perfume filled his nostrils, awakening all kinds of sensory memories. No, she was not an apparition, she was very real. "Uh, why?" he asked, sounding singularly stupid to his ears.

"I decided to take your advice and strike out on

my own, professionally. I handed in my resignation to Ramsey & Sons this morning."

"I see." He didn't though. He continued to stare at her, perplexed.

"And that left me without an office," Vanessa continued. "I happened to remember that you said you had a small conference room here which you used for staff meetings and—"

"Welcome back, boss," drawled Joan who had appeared in the doorway. "Sounds like you had quite a weekend."

"Joan and Ben helped me move my things into my new office." Vanessa smiled at the older woman.

"In case you haven't figured it out yet, her new office is our former conference room," Joan said. "She assured me that you wouldn't mind. So . . . I understand we're now a dual actuarial-and-space-planning firm. Interesting concept. One of the first of its kind, I'll wager." Casting Linc another wry glance, she sat down at her desk and busied herself with a stack of papers.

Linc caught Vanessa's arm. "I'd like to talk to you, Vanessa."

"Wouldn't you like to have some coffee and doughnuts first? Ben bought them. There are jelly-filled ones and frosted ones and— "

"Now, Vanessa." He pulled her into his own office, the largest in the small suite.

Vanessa glanced around it. "You have a lot more room than I do. Would you consider switching offices with me?"

His big hands cupped her shoulders and he turned her to face him. "Am I losing my grip on reality or have you really moved into my conference room?"

She tried to brazen it out. "I didn't think you'd mind."

"Well, I do mind. I like having a conference room. This is an actuarial firm, Vanessa. We work here, we don't play at a job."

"That's what I want to do. Work. I've had it with

play-jobs." She caught his forearms and gripped them with her fingers. "And I need an office to be taken seriously. Not my pretty pink office at Ramsey & Sons. As long as I'm in that building, with my father and brothers running things, I'll never be able to launch my career."

"I understand that, Vanessa. But what you need to do is to rent yourself an office. Office space is widely available here in Houston; you can have your choice of location, you can rent a whole floor if you choose."

She bit her lip. "I—I can't do that, Linc."

"Of course you can. You can *buy* yourself an office building."

She swallowed. "Linc, I don't know the first thing about renting—or buying—office space. I don't know the first thing about setting up an office or a business. They only thing I'm good at is interior design. At least I think I'm good at it. I think I'm an ace space planner but I've never proven myself commercially. Aside from my school record, I have no experience, no references . . ." She dropped her hands and stared at the ground. "It's—It's very hard, outlining all my inadequacies like this. My total lack of practical knowledge is humiliating. I—"

All at once he understood. "You're frightened."

That was too much for her. "No!" she insisted sharply. "My confidence may be a little shaky but—"

"Be honest with yourself, Vanessa. It's a lot shaky."

"What if I fail?" she whispered, voicing the unthinkable. "Ramseys don't fail, not ever. What if I'm the first? Suppose no one ever hires me to do anything? Oh, I wish I could boldly sashay into a realtor's office and announce that I'm going into business for myself and want to rent office space, but I just couldn't make myself do it. It's so—so public. At least here things will be private. I can take the first fumbling attempts in my career with just you looking on." She flushed and laughed slightly. "I'm not embarrassed to have you witness my first fumbling attempts in anything, you see. After all, you didn't laugh at my amateur status in sex."

Her gray eyes were enormous as she lifted them to him. She looked beautiful and vulnerable and enormously appealing. And Linc knew that this time she wasn't play-acting, this time she wasn't using her beauty to manipulate him into giving her what she wanted. She'd admitted her vulnerabilities and they were very real. She was attempting to break out of the protective Ramsey cocoon and she was scared to death.

She trusted him. He was touched by her nervous attempt to tell him so. She needed support, his support. His eyes were warm with understanding as he gazed down at her. "I suppose this firm doesn't have a pressing need for a conference room. We could always hold staff meetings in my office. The space is yours, Vanessa."

"I can work out of here, use this as my business address?" She felt elation bubble inside her and she threw herself into his arms. "Oh, Linc, I knew you'd understand! Thank you!"

He hugged her, savoring the soft warmth of her. His fingers pulled out the pins securing her chignon and her dark, thick tresses cascaded around her shoulders. Desire, sharp and swift, spun through him. And then Joan buzzed him on the intercom, bringing back the harsh realities of a Monday morning.

He had a business to run, he reminded himself. And as much as he might like to behave irresponsibly, to grab Vanessa and leave the office and all his professional responsibilities behind, he simply couldn't. He knew himself well enough to admit he didn't handle self-indulgence very gracefully.

He turned to face her, his expression grave. "There are just a few things about this arrangement that we should work out now, in the beginning, Vanessa."

He looked so serious, so somber. The quintessential actuary. Vanessa smiled. She liked his sense of order, she decided. She liked the fact that he had his own firm and worked hard. That he was sensible and upright and understanding. She even forgave him for being her father's handpicked choice of a husband for her.

"Vanessa."

She snapped to attention with a grin. "Yes, sir. Proceed."

"First, is the subject of rent. I expect you to pay something—we'll decide on a fair amount later—for the use of the office space. Second, during working hours, our personal relationship can't be allowed to interfere with our work."

"Yes, boss."

He didn't smile. "I'm not your boss, Vanessa. I'm not going to replace your father or your brothers and find busy work for you to do. You're your own boss now. Your career is your own and you can manage it without interference from me. Whatever you do with your time, be it securing clients or drawing designs or cutting out paper dolls, you're entirely on your own."

"Yes, I am." She felt lighter than air. "Finally!" The love she felt for Linc welled up within her, spreading throughout her body in a physical glow. He was willing to give her help when she asked, as with the office, but didn't demand the right to interfere as his price. He was acknowledging her as a responsible adult, with a right to freedom.

"I'm going to succeed, Linc," she promised, her gray eyes glowing. "I'll work hard, I'll submit bids and find clients and make sure I give them exactly what they're looking for."

He smiled. "I don't doubt it."

"And maybe someday, Ramsey & Sons will decide to hire me instead of their regular space planners because I'm the best in the business."

"I'm betting on it."

She fairly danced around the office, buoyant with enthusiasm. "I'll have to have a phone installed. And cards printed up."

"When I opened my firm, I mailed out announcements to everyone in the city that I'd ever met, however briefly," said Linc. "Being a Ramsey, you'll have an impressive list."

"Oh, Linc, it's so exciting. I have a million and one things to do." She laughed, her eyes bright with anticipation. "Well, I'm off. Want to meet at one for lunch?"

He restrained himself from asking where she was going. It was her business, he reminded himself. He wouldn't interfere. He reached into the pocket of his suit coat and pulled out his faithful appointment book.

"You already have me booked for lunch, remember?" she said mockingly. Actually, writing everything down made sense when one owned a business, she mused. Perhaps she should consider getting an appointment book of her own.

"And we're going to look for a ring," he announced, his tone unmistakably possessive.

"I really don't want an engagement ring, Linc," she said quickly. It was a symbol of ownership. Not to mention a tangible sign of his power over her. She loved him, but she wasn't ready to wear a ring proclaiming that yet. "Linc, I feel as if we're speeding on a runaway train. Everything is happening so fast."

Too fast. Everytime she thought of the wedding their families expected to celebrate on Saturday, panic washed over her. It was easier not to think, to put everything on hold and enjoy just this moment—the birth of her professional dream. And of Linc's encouraging support of it.

She expected him to insist on a ring and braced herself to defend her stand. But she didn't have to.

"Just lunch, then," Linc agreed. He saw the anxiety in her eyes. She was making a lot of changes in her life—her declaration of independence from her father's company was an enormous one. She didn't need any more pressure. "Where do you want to go?"

"Tio Pepe's." She named one of the more expensive Mexican restaurants in town. "My treat," she added.

She thought he might object. He didn't. He seemed to be already immersed in the files on his desk. "Linc," she said tentatively, and he glanced up. "Thanks for not insisting on a ring."

"Honey, when I buy an engagement ring for a woman, I want it to be a pleasure, not a stressor." He returned to his files.

She stood there a moment, fighting the desire to claim more of his attention. She wanted to talk about her plans for her business, she wanted to talk about rings and pleasures and stressors. His absorption in his work was disconcerting. Vanessa Ramsey was accustomed to the rapt attention of an adoring audience whenever she wanted one, regardless of whatever else the intended audience might be doing at the time.

Linc switched on his computer, his preoccupation absolute. She considered slipping onto his lap and deliberately distracting him from the numbers on the computer screen. She caught herself before she crossed the room. Linc didn't want a sexy little kitten in his office, he wanted professionalism. And so did she, Vanessa reminded herself firmly. She was in business for herself now, and she had a lot to do this morning.

She smiled as she quietly left the office. However, there was no reason why she couldn't slip onto his lap and distract him late this afternoon, when working hours were over.

Ten

Vanessa spent the next three days in a whirl of activity. Setting herself up in business involved a myriad of major tasks and minor details which could have been stressful or irritating or headache-producing, at the very least. But it wasn't, not at all. Vanessa thrived on her newfound challenge. She awakened every day with a sense of purpose; she felt charged with limitless energy.

By the end of the week, she could feel it all coming together. It might take time and patience and hard work, but she knew she was going to succeed. Her fears of professional failure faded in the light of her driving determination. For the first time in her life, she was doing what she wanted with her life and the effects were exhilarating.

Her father didn't mind that she'd left Ramsey & Sons. After all, she was safely ensconced in the same office as his carefully selected mate for her. He liked the idea that his little princess wanted to "turn her little doodles into a business." He thought it was cute, especially since she was tucked protectively under Linc's wing.

If her father only knew, Vanessa thought with a wry smile as she addressed the one hundred fifty-fourth printed announcement proclaiming the opening of Vanessa's Interiors, Inc. Linc answered whatever questions she asked him and gave her occasional pointers involving setting up a new, small business, but otherwise she was strictly on her own. He didn't check up on her or question her whereabouts. She had her own separate phone line and took her own calls. They operated as two separate and distinct entities who merely happened to be sharing the same office suite. She was not under Linc's wing. She was on her own.

And she was glad. Oh, there were times when she wished he would pay her more attention during office hours. Sometimes she wondered how a man who was so attentive and passionate with her during the evenings and nights they spent together could behave so professionally toward her during the workday.

She mocked herself for wanting it both ways—Linc's complete and undivided attention *and* his noninterference. It was a characteristic Vanessa Ramsey dilemma, she taunted herself. She'd been raised to view herself as "the cutest little trick in shoe leather," and that young miss couldn't understand a man's interest in numbers over her each and every move. Now that she had her plans for work to take seriously, she didn't take herself quite as seriously, she realized with an inward smile.

Linc paused on his way to the copier machine and glanced into his ex–conference room, now Vanessa's office and the birthplace of Vanessa's Interiors, Inc. She'd been working like a fiend all week; indeed, she reminded him of himself in his opening days of Scott Actuarial Consulting. He'd been worried that having her here would take too much of his time away from his own business, but that hadn't been the case at all. She'd come to him for occasional practical advice, but she'd otherwise managed almost everything completely on her own.

And he was glad. Oh, there were times when he wished she would pay him more attention during office hours. Sometimes he wondered how a woman who was so passionate and intensely absorbed with him during the evenings and nights they spent together could adopt such a thoroughly professional demeanor toward him during the workday.

He mocked himself for wanting it both ways—Vanessa's complete and undivided attention and being left alone to pursue his work. He had been the one to point out that their professional and private lives must be separate, and now he felt himself wishing they'd overlap a bit. He wanted to know where she was going when she left the office. He wanted to know about all those phone calls she was making and getting.

It was a characteristic Lincoln Scott dilemma, he taunted himself. He advised his family in business as well as personal matters. He'd grown accustomed to their dependence. He frowned thoughtfully. Though he appreciated Vanessa's independence, he was going to have to be on guard against attempting to take over for her. She would not appreciate that, not after a lifetime with take-charge Ramseys.

Vanessa looked up and caught Linc staring at her. She smiled. "Hi. I didn't know you were in yet."

He looked a little sheepish. "I arrived ten minutes ago. Joan informed me rather tartly that you were the first one in again this morning and that you bought the doughnuts for the third time. She was quick to point out that I haven't bought them once this week."

"Shame on you, Lincoln Scott. I'm afraid your frenetic social life is starting to interfere with your work," Vanessa teased.

Linc groaned. "If I didn't know how much your parents adore me, I'd begin to suspect that they're trying to kill me with socializing. A party every night this week! I'm a quiet, staid, conservative actuary, not a reveling socialite."

"And then there are those wild, late nights *after* the party with the Ramseys' insatiable daughter. Poor Lincoln! These are trying times for a diligent, early-to-bed, early-to-rise farm boy from Kansas."

Linc strode into her small office and dragged her to her feet. She laughed up at him. Maybe it was time their professional and personal lives mingled, just a little, he decided. "I'd like to go early-to-bed with the Ramseys' insatiable daughter. I think I'm up for the challenge."

She was delighted with his advance. After all, there was no reason that their nighttime relationship should be entirely separate from their daytime one. She slipped into his arms and moved provocatively against him. "Mmm, I know you are." Lifting her head, she brushed her lips against his mouth.

He savored the supple, feminine curves pressed against him, and tightened his arms around her. Not so many hours ago, she'd lain naked and pliant and moaning in his arms as they'd scaled rapturous heights they had never achieved before.

"Last night was fantastic, Linc," she whispered, as if divining his thoughts.

"Each time with you is better than the last, Vanessa. Each time there is more meaning, more passion, more lo—"

"More love?" she was quick to pick up on his lapse. Why wouldn't he say it? Because he didn't love her? Or because he didn't want to risk saying it first. She gazed up at him, her eyes soft with love. She'd been doing a lot of risk-taking, business-wise, these past few days. Perhaps it was time to take an emotional risk as well. She drew up all her courage and forged ahead. "I love you, Linc. I—I think you know that."

He smiled slightly. "Yet you won't accept an engagement ring from me and you won't discuss our wedding—which is scheduled for tomorrow afternoon."

She stirred uncomfortably and avoided meeting his gaze.

"I've noticed the way you change the subject any time the wedding is mentioned. You've partied all week with our families, but whenever the wedding is mentioned, you deftly but inevitably switch to another topic of conversation."

Vanessa gulped. It was true, but she hadn't thought she had been that obvious.

"I think it's clear that if we're to be together at all, we should be married, Vanessa," Linc persisted. He couldn't seem to stop himself. He wanted to give her the time and the distance she needed and yet he also wanted to bind her to him in every possible way. Emotionally, physically, *and* legally. He loved her and wanted to marry her; the wedding couldn't come too soon for him. It was a damnable paradox, he silently lamented.

"Yes, but Linc," she began and was interrupted by a buzz on the intercom.

"Vanessa, you have a visitor." Joan's voice sounded over the intercom. She had agreed to serve as Vanessa's receptionist, too. "He's carrying a tree and he says he's your brother."

Vanessa slipped away from Linc. Slade Ramsey joined them a half-minute later, a four-foot ficus tree in his arms. "I brought you an office-warming gift," he said, setting down the tree. He glanced around the small office. "Too bad you don't have any windows in here. The tree would do better with natural light."

"Linc, knock out that wall and put in a bay window," Vanessa ordered.

Slade looked as if he expected Linc instantly to comply. Linc and Vanessa exchanged grins.

Slade stared from one to the other, then asked. "Vanessa, could I talk to you for a few minutes?" He politely did not add "alone," but Linc picked up on the implied request.

"I have some calls to return," he said and left her office, closing the door behind him.

Vanessa and Slade faced each other. "I like the tree," she said tentatively. And couldn't resist adding, "Did Daddy send you down to check out my cute little office? You'll have to tell him that it's not decorated with rainbow and hearts wallpaper and I don't have a pink princess phone."

"He'll be sorely disappointed," Slade said dryly. His eyes met hers. "Rad thinks it's a good idea, your going off on your own in space planning and interior design." He gazed at his sister and added, a little awkwardly, "I didn't know how unhappy you were with the company until Rad told me, Vanessa. I guess I've continued to think of you as a fun-and-games little co-ed, majoring in partying."

She had never been that, Vanessa thought, but avoided the impulse to snap it at him, thus launching another Ramsey verbal slugfest. "It's nice of you to come down here and wish me success, Slade," she said instead.

Her words seemed to touch Slade, unleashing a sudden, fierce burst of emotion in him. "Oh, Vanessa, I've been so worried about you!" He caught both her hands and clutched them in his. "This wedding of yours tomorrow—it's all happening so fast! And with the entire Harrison clan around until all hours every night, none of us have had a chance to talk about what's really going on, Vanessa."

"And what's that, Slade?"

"Vanessa, you don't have to play dumb with me. This is your big brother Slade you're talking to, remember? We've had our differences over the years— in fact, there've been times when I've wanted to throttle you—but I thought, I hoped, you knew that you could always come to me whenever you were in trouble."

"If you're talking about Jed's extortion plot—"

"What extortion plot? Vanessa, I'm talking about this wedding of yours which has been so hastily set for tomorrow. Are you one hundred percent sure that you want to go through with it? Be honest with me, honey."

She was silent for a long moment. And then: "No, Slade, I'm not one hundred percent sure."

"I thought that might be the case. And, Vanessa,

I'm here to tell you that you don't have to marry Lincoln Scott tomorrow. I understand that you must have panicked when you learned you were pregnant and—"

"You think I'm marrying Lincoln because I'm pregnant?"

He smiled at her, gently, compassionately. "Vanessa, I know how easy it is to be carried away, to—uh—forget—certain necessities." He blushed slightly. "Did I tell you that Shavonne is pregnant again? A little sooner than we'd planned, but as I was saying—"

"You know how easy it is to be carried away and to forget certain necessities," Vanessa finished for him, her gray eyes sparkling. She hugged him. "Congratulations to you and Shavonne and Robin, Slade. I hope this one will be a boy, a little Slade Junior."

"Thanks, but let's not get sidetracked, Vanessa. The issue at hand is *your* pregnancy and whether or not you have to marry Lincoln Scott tomorrow because of it."

"I had no idea how inventive and imaginative my three older brothers could be," Vanessa said lightly. First, Rad had assumed that she'd wanted to elope with Linc, then Jed had decided that she was making herself the supreme sacrifice in a dastardly blackmail scheme, now Slade was convinced she was pregnant. "Slade, I appreciate your concern, but—"

"Vanessa, I can guess how you must feel. Trapped. Scared. You're afraid to back out, what with Dad and Mother and all the Harrisons preparing for a wedding tomorrow afternoon."

'That's partially true, but—"

"I'm here to offer you an alternative, Vanessa. It's taken me all week to come up with one, but here it is. If you really don't want to go through with the wedding, come over to my house tonight. I have the keys to the boat. You and Shavonne and Robin and I will go out for a long weekend cruise. I'll send back a ship-to-shore message, advising the others of our safety but not our whereabouts. By the time we return to the marina on Tuesday, the pressure will be off. The Harrisons will have been dispatched back to Kansas and the wedding canceled. I'll take the heat from the folks. I'll claim I kidnapped you, if need be. And you can have the time you need to decide what you really want to do with your life."

Vanessa listened, diverted by his plan. She could almost visualize it happening, but with some other woman playing the kidnapped, pregnant heiress. Tara Brady would be an interesting choice for the role. Perhaps Melinda Sue Harper. But not herself. She'd outgrown her interest in deceptive games, she realized with a smile. "Slade, I'm deeply touched that you've dreamed up this wonderful scheme, but it has one big flaw. I'm not pregnant."

Slade cast her a disbelieving glance. "The Ramsey pride can be crippling in times of emotional crisis, Vanessa. Nobody knows that better than I."

How did one Ramsey convince another that he was dead wrong? Vanessa mused. Especially when that Ramsey was absolutely determined to believe he was right. She sighed. It seemed like an exercise in futility. Wouldn't it be more expedient to tactfully send him on his way and resume her business at hand?

She stood on tiptoe and kissed his cheek. "Thank you for everything, Slade. I'll certainly keep your offer in mind."

"Vanessa, you're my baby sister. I'd do anything in the world for you, always remember that. And if you feel the need to escape from your situation—"

"You'll be there to provide the means." She took his arm. "Slade, I don't know if I've ever told you so before, but you're a great brother. I know there have been times in the past when I've said some things to you that were downright nasty, but I want you to know that I—I never really meant any of them."

"Ah, Vanessa, I always knew that." He gave her a quick, hard hug, then strode briskly from the office.

Linc sauntered in a few minutes later. "I saw Slade

tear out of here looking like a prophet of gloom," he remarked casually. "Is something wrong?"

Vanessa shrugged. "From Slade's point of view there is. He thinks I'm pregnant, and that you and my parents have formed an unholy alliance to force me into marrying you."

Linc winced. "I thought Jed was the one who'd come up with that particular reason for our marriage."

"Oh, no, Jed has gone one better. He's convinced that you're blackmailing Daddy and that our marriage is part of the extortion package," Vanessa said dryly.

"Blackmail!" Linc was appalled by the misapprehension. "Vanessa, I think we should assure your brothers that—"

"I've already denied the blackmail scheme and the pregnancy, Linc. Neither one of them believes me. There's only one sure way to convince the both of them that they're wrong on all counts."

He narrowed his brows. "And what's that?"

She gazed at him steadily. "To call off the wedding tomorrow," she murmured softly, and held her breath.

"Call off the wedding?" Linc stared at the ground for a long moment. And then he raised his eyes to hers. "Is that what you really want, Vanessa?"

Vanessa gulped. This had to be the most disconcerting moment of her entire life, she thought dismally, easily supplanting the previously most disconcerting moment, when Troy Timmons had confirmed his homosexuality to her. But this was far worse because she loved Linc. She was both physically and emotionally involved with him. She couldn't imagine another man being as understanding and patient and loving with the nervous virgin she had been. Hadn't he helped her discover the joyful and spontaneous nature of her own sexuality?

And would she have had the courage to break out of that suffocating pseudo-job at Ramsey & Sons without his support? She thought not. Didn't she owe him something for that? But did she owe him a wedding one week after they'd met?

"Linc, I love you." She felt hot tears gather in her eyes. "But we've only known each other a week. I—I just don't see why we have to rush into marriage so soon. After all, you aren't blackmailing my father and I'm not pregnant. It was high-handed and manipulative of Daddy to cart your whole family down here to force us into a wedding, but we don't have to cave in to it, do we?"

"No," Linc said quietly. "But then, I never felt I was caving in to your father by marrying you. It's what I wanted, too. And when he scheduled the wedding for Saturday, I was delighted to go along with him. I guess I was being just as high-handed and manipulative as he was. I have no doubts about us, Vanessa, but it's only fair that you should be given the time to reach that conclusion on your own."

Vanessa stared at the carpet, pain and sadness sweeping through her in a great wave. "I want time, Linc, I need it. I don't want to hurt you or disappoint your family or mine, but I don't want to rush into marriage with a man I've known only a week, even if that man is you. I warned you that I'm actually very cautious and controlled. I've read too many books about whirlwind courtships ending in disastrous marriages. The bestseller list abounds with titles about the dangers of disparate couples plunging blindly into a relationship that ends up hurting them both. I don't want to—to find myself enrolled in a How To Save Your Marriage workshop a year from now." Her lower lip quivered. She felt as if she were going to cry.

Linc crossed the room in two great strides and swept her into his arms. "Vanessa, it's all right. I understand."

She drew back a little to look up at him. "You do?" she whispered.

"I love you, Vanessa." He gazed down at her, his

blue eyes warm. "And I want you to be happy. I want you to marry me, but I also want you to be sure it's what *you* want. There really is no reason why we have to get married this Saturday other than the fact that your father decreed it. If you'd like, I'll explain to my family that we're postponing the wedding. And I'll talk to your parents, too, if you want me to."

She gasped. "You'd do that for me? You—You don't hate me?"

"Honey, I just told you that I love you."

"I thought you'd issue an ultimatum. Something along the lines of 'marry me this Saturday or I'll never see you again.' " She gave a sad little sniff.

"Not a chance. Ultimatums don't seem to work for me where you're concerned. Remember my alleged vow to keep my hands off you until after the wedding? That one went down in flames shortly after I made it." He smiled and lightly stroked her hair. "I'd never refuse to see you again, Vanessa. There's no way I could ever follow through on such a threat."

"Linc, I don't want to lose you," she said with a soft sob.

"You're not going to, sweetheart. I intend to begin courting you intensely. And this time you'll be the one to set the wedding date whenever you feel as sure of our future together as I am."

She clung to him, aching with love, her anxiety slowly melting. "You're the most generous, understanding, and—and confident man I've ever met."

"I'm a gem," agreed Linc. "I have no doubts you'll hang on to me."

She laughed, feeling giddy with an overwhelming sense of relief. She wasn't going to be rushed into a wedding tomorrow and she wasn't going to lose Linc because of it. "So this is what it means to have your cake and eat it, too!" She sighed happily. "Oh, Linc, I love you!"

He kissed her. "I love you, too, sweetheart. Now, let's set the scene here. We're no longer an engaged couple who are to be married tomorrow, but a couple who've just met one week ago. I'd like to ask you for a date for tomorrow night. Uh, dinner and a movie?"

"I'd love to."

"Good. I'll pick you up at six."

"Linc? What about tonight? I, er—happen to be free."

"I'll spend tonight with my family at the hotel. It'll be their last night in Houston and I want to explain things to them. I don't think you want to join us for that."

Her cheeks flushed a deep pink. "No, I suppose I don't. Linc, do you think they'll hate me? I don't want that to happen."

"They won't hate you," he said. "I'll tell them that it's our mutual decision to postpone the wedding. My family won't question me, they always assume that I'm doing the right thing." He kissed the top of her head. "Now stop worrying, honey. Spend a quiet evening and go to bed early tonight. I intend to, as soon as I get back to my place from the hotel. After the round of festivities we've been through this past week, we need a night off."

"I could come over to your apartment after you've talked to your family. We could go to bed as early as you want," she offered, moving seductively against him.

Linc groaned. "Sweetheart, don't tempt me. It's better if you stay home tonight. I'll call you when I get in, okay?"

"No, it's not okay," she grumbled. "You know how I hate not getting my own way." But her smile took the bite from her words.

"I'll call you tonight," Linc repeated, and then began to laugh.

Vanessa stared at him. "What's so funny?" she asked curiously.

"You, enrolled in a How To Save Your Marriage workshop," said Linc.

She joined in his laughter. Yes, that was a hilariously exaggerated fear, for Linc would never hurt her, she knew that now. He'd told her that he loved her and she believed him. A man like Linc didn't use those words lightly. Vanessa hugged him, her gray eyes shining with love. Her love for him would bring her happiness, not pain.

Eleven

By ten o'clock that evening, a restless and bored Vanessa was pacing the floor of her bedroom. Her parents hadn't taken the cancellation of her wedding well. They'd ranted and pleaded, they'd bribed and threatened. But ultimately, they could do nothing because Vanessa had assured them that she intended to continue her relationship with Linc and that the two of them planned to marry in their own sweet time.

She called her brothers Rad and Slade to tell them the news, but was unable to reach Jed. Her parents could tell Ricky, Vanessa decided, as she retired to her room. There, she tried to interest herself in the stack of new books she'd received last week from her book clubs.

It proved an impossible task. Vanessa put down her book when she realized that she'd read the same paragraph six times and still didn't remember what it said. Her attention kept wandering from the printed page as visions of Linc were superimposed on her mind's eye. She endlessly reviewed their conversation this morning in his office. He had been so understanding, so patient and kind. Tears blurred in her eyes. She hoped she hadn't caused him pain by canceling their wedding. No, she quickly corrected herself, postponing it.

Her heart turned over in her chest. She had made

it clear to Linc that this was simply a temporary delay, hadn't she? He did understand that she really loved him and wanted to marry him—but at a later date—didn't he?

Suddenly her mind seemed to go blank. She couldn't remember exactly what she had said to him other than wanting to call off the wedding tomorrow. She couldn't remember the expression on his face when he'd agreed with her. Had he been devastated, but tried to hide it from her? If so, it surely would've shown in his eyes. She tried to remember if his eyes had reflected devastating pain and to her growing panic, she couldn't seem to recall. What if he had been deeply hurt and she'd been too self-involved with her own relief to see? It wouldn't be the first time she'd been too self-involved to recognize someone else's misery, she reminded herself darkly.

She felt her throat tighten and her stomach lurched. If she hadn't been aware that he'd been hurt, she undoubtedly wouldn't have noticed if he'd been angry, either. Suppose he had been furious with her and she hadn't even realized it? What if he were so angry that he refused to see her again? She vaguely remembered voicing such a fear, and that he had reassured her. But had she missed the underlying edge in his voice? Had she been hearing only what she wanted to hear?

Vanessa paled. She'd watched her father and brothers use the single-minded preoccupations of others to their own advantage for years! The Ramseys' silkily reassuring words held an underlying meaning only for those sharp enough to discern it. Those who foolishly heard only what suited them inevitably lost out.

Suddenly the fact that Linc hadn't insisted on seeing her tonight loomed ominously. Vanessa gulped. She forced herself to examine the situation from an outsider's point of view. For example, what would be

Melinda Sue Harper's reaction to this latest bit of Ramsey gossip?

Vanessa winced. She'd chosen to consider the wrong person's imaginary viewpoint. "Of course Linc wouldn't want to see you tonight," Melinda Sue would say gleefully. "After humilating himself by telling his family that his wedding was off, do you actually believe he'd want to see *you*, the cause of it all? Only a vain, conceited idiot could even come up with such an idea!"

Vanessa felt a sudden thrill of fear. Oh Lord, could that possibly be true? Had she hurt and humiliated Linc and then expected him to tell her that it didn't matter, that he loved her in spite of it? She *was* a vain, conceited idiot!

She threw a light jacket over her plum silk Oriental-style lounging pajamas and rushed from the room to the garage, blessing her father's custom of always keeping the car keys in all the cars. She hopped into her mother's silver-gray Mercedes 560SEC and sped to Linc's apartment. She had to tell him that she loved him, she thought frantically. She must make it absolutely clear that he was the only man in the world for her.

As she pulled into the parking area of his apartment complex, Vanessa faced the truth. She wasn't here only to reassure Linc of her love, she admitted to herself. She was here for reassurance that he loved her, too.

Linc had given her a key to his apartment earlier in the week and she fitted it into the front door. The living room was dark and she crept stealthily toward the light coming from the bedroom door which stood ajar.

"Linc!"

She was so stunned by the sound of the feminine voice calling his name, that for a split second, Vanessa thought she had been the one who'd uttered it, knowing all the while that she hadn't, of course.

She fairly raced those few short steps to the bedroom and then stopped dead in her tracks at the threshold. For Linc was standing at the foot of the bed, his back to her, and on the bed . . . Vanessa blinked, then stared with shocked gray eyes. On the bed, lying languidly in a come-hitherish sprawl, dressed in the briefest, most explicit black lace teddy that she'd ever seen, was Lexie Madison.

"Hi, Linc," Lexie crooned breathily. She shifted, showing her long legs to full advantage. Long, shapely legs encased in black spike heels and dark seamed stockings attached to garters.

Vanessa couldn't stifle the small, choking sound which escaped from her throat. Linc whirled round to face her. "Vanessa!" He appeared as dazed and as stunned as she was.

Lexie gave a nervous giggle. "Looks like we were caught in the act. You weren't supposed to show up tonight, Vanessa."

"Obviously," Vanessa managed to say before she turned and fled from the apartment. She heard a voice calling to her, but she didn't look back. She heard footsteps pursuing her and she ran faster.

"You weren't supposed to show up tonight, Vanessa." Lexie's voice kept ringing in her ears. Of course she wasn't! So that was why Linc had insisted that she stay home tonight! He had been angry with her for calling off the wedding, unforgivably, vengefully angry. She wondered when he had called Lexie and set up tonight's tryst. Immediately after he'd assured her that he planned a quiet evening alone? Or had telling his family been the impetus for his call to Lexie? Was a fling with another woman necessary to soothe his wounded masculine pride?

She was panting and trembling, hot, thick tears streaming down her cheeks by the time she reached her mother's car. "Vanessa, wait!" came a panicked male voice. It sounded like her brother Jed, she thought, but immediately dismissed the possibility. A shock-induced numbness settled over her.

She slipped into the car and started the engine.

As she was pulling out, she saw that it was Jed waving frantically and calling to her. She stared at him. What was Jed doing here? she wondered vaguely.

"Vanessa, wait! You can't drive in the shape you're in!" He was shouting.

The shape she was in . . . Vanessa guessed what she must look like, running around the parking lot in her pajamas, her hair wild, her face red and tear-stained. She decided that whatever unfortunate coincidence had placed Jed here wasn't worth looking into at this particular time. She was an emotional wreck and too likely to blurt out what she'd just seen in Linc's apartment. And that was a piece of information that she never intended to share with anybody, especially not her brother Jed.

She drove past him and kept on driving. Over miles of freeway, for nearly a half hour. After a few near-misses, she decided that she was a menace on the roadway and owed it to the other drivers to get off. But where could she go? She didn't want to go home yet, nor could she imagine facing any of her brothers or any of her friends. The only person she'd ever allowed to see her in such an emotional state was Linc.

She stifled a sob. It was depressingly ironic that the only person with whom she felt able to share her pain was the very one who'd caused it.

She exited the freeway and drove through the city streets. Eventually, the bright lights of a convenience store drew her in. She felt an incredible craving for coffee, black and hot and strong. Ignoring the leers and shrill wolf whistles from two young men sitting in a pickup truck parked alongside her, Vanessa went into the store. She purchased a large Styrofoam cup of coffee and carried it back to the car.

She gulped down half of it, burning her tongue and her throat, and not caring. The brief, physical pain was actually a welcome diversion from her far more intense emotional suffering. She leaned her head back against the headrest and closed her eyes. The coffee was strong, all right, it had probably been brewing for hours. Within minutes, she could feel the jolt of caffeine surge through her bloodstream. She drank more.

By the time she'd finished the coffee, a remarkable change had taken place in her. Her brain had been cleared of the blinding hysteria which had driven her from Linc's apartment, and her mind was beginning to work again. Vanessa sat up abruptly.

Her mind was racing as she fitted together seemingly incongruous snippets from the interlude in Linc's apartment. Linc had been fully dressed and standing at the foot of his bed, she recalled, while Lexie posed like a centerfold candidate on it. It was an incriminating scene, for sure, *but* . . .

Vanessa stared absently at a customer removing a bag of ice from the outdoor dispensing machine. Thinking rationally now, such a setup simply didn't seem in character for Linc and what she knew him to be. Oh, there were endless tales of women being deceived sexually by men *but* she had a complete dossier on his sexual history and knew he had practiced no such deceptions in the past. There was always a first time, *but* . . .

Not for Linc, Vanessa decided, suddenly surer than she'd ever been of anything. Only this morning he had told her that he loved her and wanted to marry her. He was a man of his word, a man of character. He had always been honest with her, even when it would have been easier—and to his own advantage—to have deceived her. Whatever Sexy Lexie was doing in that bed—*with her shoes on!*—Vanessa now was convinced that Linc had no part in getting her there.

A setup. The phrase came back to her in a newfound light—along with a certain coincidence which suddenly didn't seem like a coincidence at all! What *was* her brother Jed doing at Linc's apartment complex? She'd been too upset at the time to question it. But she was thinking clearly now, and if Linc wasn't guilty of cheating on her, then Jed's presence at that particular time and place was much more than a coincidence.

It was a setup!

Vanessa started the engine and pulled out of the parking lot at breakneck speed. She saw it all now. Jed had conspired with Lexie to set up Linc in a compromising position. Damn, it was the staple of every soap opera, both daytime and prime time. Why hadn't she realized it sooner?

Of course, the co-conspirators couldn't have known that Vanessa would arrive at such an opportune moment, so they must have had other means for providing the incriminating evidence. A camera, naturally. After all, the Ramseys were photographically inclined. And Jed owned a Polaroid, whose pictures were instantly developed and available on the spot.

Vanessa pressed her lips together tightly and drove faster. Jed must have planned to take pictures of Lexie lunging at Linc and then rush over to River Oaks to show them to the folks. Undisputed evidence, however erroneous, of the bridegroom-to-be cavorting with sexy, scantily clad Lexie in flagrante delicto the night before the wedding. What else could Quentin Ramsey do but make the necessary cancellations?

Vanessa arrived back at Linc's apartment in record time. The pieces of the puzzle had all fallen neatly into place. She'd been unable to tell her brother of her change in wedding plans and Jed, still operating under his ridiculous blackmail theory, had attempted some blackmail of his own. And Lexie Madison would be the ideal choice to participate in such a scheme. She was theatrical and vindictive and eager to even the score with any Ramsey. Vanessa shivered. It was hard to believe that her sweet brother Slade had ever been engaged to that creature, but that was ancient history and she supposed that stranger things had happened.

Like her father commissioning a husband for her.

For the first time since she'd left her house that night, Vanessa smiled.

She fairly flew up the stairs to Linc's apartment and let herself in with her key. Linc was sitting on the sofa, holding a ceramic mug between his hands and staring sightlessly at the screen of the television set on which an announcer was cheerfully discussing weather patterns.

She switched the TV off. Linc set down the mug and stood up, his eyes fixed on her.

"Hello, Vanessa," he said quietly.

"I—I'm back," she said unnecessarily. She felt nervous and high-strung and perilously close to tears again.

He made no move toward her, and a tense silence stretched between them for several interminable seconds. "I made some coffee," Linc said at last. "Would you like some?"

"I just finished a pint of high-voltage coffee myself," she said softly, her voice shaky. "Whatever the negative publicity about caffeine, it gave me the buzz necessary to jolt my brain into working again. Of course, I probably won't sleep for the next thirty-six hours." She gave a short, nervous laugh.

"Jed and Lexie are gone," Linc said. "But before they went, I made each of them give me their motives for staging that bedroom farce tonight. And that's what it was, Vanessa. A staged—"

"Linc, don't!" Casting off all inhibitions, she ran to him and threw her arms around him. "I know it was staged. Please don't think that you have to give me an explanation. I believe in you. I trust you. And I know that you had nothing to do with that floozy turning up in your bed in one of Frederick's of Hollywood's raunchier ensembles."

Linc gave a strangled laugh. "Ah, Vanessa, there's no one like you." He held her tightly, as if he would never let her go. "I was as shocked as you were to see Lexie Madison in my bed tonight, Vanessa. I'd just come back from the hotel, walked into my bedroom and switched on the light and—"

"—there was that red-headed weasel just waiting to entrap you," Vanessa said hotly. "My idiot brother must've been lurking on the premises with his Polaroid camera, too."

"He was in the bathroom. You arrived at the apartment just a few seconds after I did, Vanessa. Jed hadn't had the chance to take a picture yet. When you ran away, he followed you out the door. I tried to follow, too, but first I had to break loose from that female octopus who had a stranglehold on me. By the time I made it to the parking lot, you were pulling out." His lips brushed her temple as his hands tenderly caressed her. "At that moment, I could've easily killed both Jed and Lexie for what they'd done to us. Vanessa. the look on your face when you saw that woman on the bed . . ." His voice deepened and trailed off and he crushed her against him. "You looked so hurt, so betrayed. God, Vanessa, I'd never do anything to hurt you that way. I love you so much."

"I know," she whispered, snuggling deeper in his arms. "It just took me a little while to remember, that's all."

He bent his head and kissed her, lightly at first, then with increasing passion. Vanessa felt the swift, sensuous heat ignite her every nerve. She was engulfed in the sweetly tempestuous sensations which only his touch could evoke. She touched him, her mouth open and hungry on his, as the luxuriant warmth spread through her.

When Linc picked her up and carried her into the bedroom, she felt a stunning, almost overwhelming surge of desire, of need. They quickly shed their clothes and tumbled onto the bed together, breathless, then laughed at their incredible urgency.

"I love you, Linc," Vanessa told him, over and over, exulting in the words and savoring each and every kiss and caress they shared. Those Jed-induced doubts she'd had to face tonight had had the effect of strengthening her love for him and affirming her faith and trust in him. "Linc, I'll marry you tomorrow if you'd like," she added, gazing into his eyes as she lay in his arms.

"I know you would, my love," he said softly, kissing her with lingering sweetness. "But let's stick to the plan we worked out in the office this morning. We'll have a very romantic courtship and whatever kind of wedding we want whenever we want it."

"And in the meantime, we'll be engaged. And we'll shop for a ring tomorrow, Linc. It'll be a pleasure, not a stressor," she added, remembering his words. "And it'll mean that you're off limits to every woman but me." Visible symbols of possession and belonging were fine between independent and equal adults, she decided happily.

"We're definitely both off limits to everyone but each other," Linc agreed lovingly, as his body merged with hers.

Closing her eyes, Vanessa thrilled to the feel of him within her, full and strong and unyielding, and she instinctively sought to draw him in deeper. They moved together, intrinsically joined, as passion wove a timeless spell around them, uniting their bodies and souls in a bond of loving rapture. They lost themselves in each other, soaring to exquisite heights of pleasure until both let go and were flung together into a boundless chasm of sensual ecstasy.

It wasn't until a long time later, as they lay pleasantly and languidly weary in the aftermath of that voluptuous burst of passion that Vanessa reopened the subject of Lexie and Jed and their ill-fated setup.

"I know that Jed, in his own off-the-wall way, was trying to be gallant, to prevent me from being the payoff in his imaginary extortion plot," she said with a wry shake of her head. "But how did he get Lexie to cooperate? Somehow I don't see him telling Lexie that he thought Dad was being blackmailed. Jed's got too much Ramsey pride to disclose anything that sleazy about the family to an outsider."

"You're right, he kept his blackmail theory to himself." Linc propped himself up on one elbow and gazed down at her. "He told Lexie that he wanted to play a practical joke on the two of us. Something similar to a stripper popping out of a cake at a bachelor party and then jumping into the honoree's lap, he said. There wasn't going to be any bachelor party or cake or stripper, but Lexie could help him pull off a reasonable facsimile of the gag."

"By wearing that costume and assaulting you in your bedroom while Jed recorded the hilarity on film. Which would conveniently develop inside the camera within sixty seconds," Vanessa finished indignantly. "How did they get into your apartment?"

"Oh, your brother is a detail man with plenty of foresight. He lifted my key during one of the parties this week, slipped out and had a copy made, then returned it, without me ever being the wiser."

"It sounds like a typical Jed stunt," Vanessa said crossly. "I can see why Lexie didn't question it. And of course, she'd leap at the chance to—quote—play a funny little joke—end quote—on me."

"That's exactly what she said!" marveled Linc. He raised his voice to a ridiculous falsetto and batted his eyelashes in a rather dreadful imitation of Lexie, " 'Why, I never meant to upset Vanessa. Jed and I were just playing a funny little joke on her.' "

"Ohh!" Vanessa heaved an exasperated groan. "I'd like to take the pair of them and—and—" she paused, pondering a suitably horrific fate.

Linc smiled at her. "After I sent Lexie on her way— she did have a dress with her, thankfully—I explained to Jed that we'd decided to postpone the wedding. We talked for a while and I think I convinced him that I'm not involved in some nefarious scheme. He seemed almost apologetic by the time he left."

"Almost?" Vanessa scowled. "To paraphrase, being Jed Ramsey means never having to say you're sorry."

"Don't be too hard on him, honey." Linc leaned down and kissed her. She was smiling dreamily when he lifted his lips from a tender and passionate kiss later. "Nothing or no one can ever come between us."

'We'll always be open and honest with each other," Vanessa vowed, lacing her arms around his neck. "No secrets, no deceptions, no dossiers. We'll always have access to all the intimate details about each other."

"Always," Linc promised, sealing their pledge of faith with a kiss.

Epilogue

Six months later, a nervous trio of female Ramseys crowded around a magnificently gowned Vanessa in the small back room of the church. The organ music swelled and filled the air. Vanessa's four brothers, tall and handsome in their gray morning suits, ushered the arriving guests down the aisle to the pews. Sitting in several beribboned pews at the front of the church were the Harrisons, all nineteen of them, who'd flown in from Kansas two days before.

"Courtney," Erin Ramsey ordered her small daughter, "stand still while I fix your bow. Carrie Beth, come here, I have to retie your sash." She ministered to the girls with one hand, her other arm full of year-old Connor, who was rather rakishly swigging juice from his bottle.

"I just know that Robin will balk at going down the aisle," lamented a visibly pregnant Shavonne Ramsey. "Oh Lord, now she's mangling her nosegay!" She rushed over to rescue the flowers from the toddler's enthusiastic grip.

"Now, let's go through it one more time, Vanessa," an anxious Nola Ramsey urged her daughter. "I'm to walk down the aisle with Jed and Ricky. The other boys will already be at the front of the church and, of course, Daddy will walk you down. Straighten your veil a little, sweetie. Oh, Vanessa!" The Mother of the Bride reached into her embroidered handbag and delicately sniffed into her lace handkerchief. "I've never seen you look more beautiful!"

"Thanks, Mama," said Vanessa. She smiled at her tearful mother, she grinned at her nervous sisters-in-law and she laughed out loud at the antics of her active nieces and nephew. She was gloriously serene, exempt from even a mild case of the bridal jitters.

In just a few moments she would become Mrs. Lincoln Scott and she had never been happier or more at peace with herself and the world. Waiting these six months had been a wise choice, for she and Linc had utilized that time to really get to know each other, to deepen and strengthen the bonds they'd already forged between them.

She loved being with him. No matter where they were or what they were doing, whether alone or with others, their eyes would meet and they would smile in joint recognition of the shared moment of intimacy. They had private jokes and secret smiles and understood each other in a way no one else ever had.

"Vanessa, you're not even nervous!" breathed Erin, shifting baby Connor to her other hip while she glanced askance at the three little girls chasing each other around the room. Lace and ribbons and ruffles were flying, along with flower petals and ferns. "I'm a wreck. I'm terrified these kids will turn your wedding into a free-for-all."

Vanessa smiled placidly and shrugged. "Stop worrying, Erin. Let the kids have a good time. It's our wedding, and Linc and I want everyone to enjoy themselves. We certainly intend to."

There had been a time when Erin would've been right to worry about the effect of the children's behavior upon her, Vanessa knew, but those days of high-strung, nervous edginess were over. She had outlets for all that repressed energy of hers now. Vanessa's lips curved into a soft smile. There was Linc, of course. No woman could be a seething mass of self-centered frustration with a man like Linc to love.

And she had her work as a creative source of satisfaction. She'd already sketched designs for several clients and was looking forward to her first contract outside the Houston area. It wouldn't be long before she'd be submitting her space-planning designs to national companies. The commissions she'd earned had given her the confidence to rent an office of her own on the floor above Linc's office. With her growing list of clients, she would soon be hiring her own secretary-receptionist.

There was a knock at the door and Rad and Slade appeared to escort their wives down the aisle.

"Here's Uncle Jed and Uncle Rick. You go next, Grandma," six-year-old Carrie Beth instructed her grandmother who was once again dabbing at her eyes.

"Such a beautiful bride," Nola said with a dainty sniff. "Such a beautiful family. I'm so very proud of all of you." She departed on the arms of her two younger sons.

"I'll walk Courtney and Robin down the aisle, Aunt Vanessa," Carrie Beth said calmly. "Don't worry. We'll be good."

"Of course you will," said Vanessa, stooping to give the little girl a hug. "And don't forget to smile for the video-cam and the photographers."

She guided her nieces out of the room and took her father's arm at the head of the aisle.

"You look like a queen, Vanessa," Quentin said softly. Tears gathered in his steel-gray eyes. "I can hardly believe it—my baby girl, all grown up." His voice was wistful. "Lord, it seems like only yesterday that you were as tiny as those little ladies." He looked at the three flower girls who were waltzing down the aisle ahead of them, beaming at the onlookers, as if they did this sort of thing every day.

Linc was standing at the altar. He had turned when the wedding march began and was watching Vanessa walk down the aisle to him. Their gazes met and they smiled at each other, their eyes bright with love and promises.

THE EDITOR'S CORNER

At LOVESWEPT, we believe that the settings for our books can be Anywhere, USA, but we do like to be transported into the lives of the hero and heroine, and into their worlds, and we enjoy it very much when our authors create authentic small town or big city settings for their delicious love stories. This month we'll take you from a farm in Oklahoma, to a resort town on the ocean in New Jersey, to the big cities of Los Angeles, New York, and Chicago, so settle into your favorite traveling armchair and enjoy these new places and new couples in love.

Fran Baker has done a wonderful job recreating the world of the farmer and oilman in **THE WIDOW AND THE WILDCATTER,** #246, a heartwarming and heartwrenching story of love, family, and land. Chance McCoy is a hero you'll love to love. He's strong, gorgeous, adventurous, and available to the woman who needs him to make her and her grandfather's dream come true. What begins as a dream to strike it rich ends as dreams of love are fulfilled for Chance and Joni. Fran Baker certainly does strike it rich in this story!

With our next title, we leave the farmlands of Oklahoma for the New Jersey shore where Cass Lindley, heroine of **SILK ON THE SKIN,** LOVESWEPT #247, owns an exclusive boutique in a resort town, and is the major stockholder of the family's lingerie business. Cass has her hands full of silks, satin, and lace when she discovers that her company is in trouble. M&L Lingerie creates the finest intimate garments for the market but the chairman of the board, Ned Marks, decides they should compete with Fredrick's of Hollywood! Cass is appalled and finally listens to the new president, Dallas Carter, who has a plan to oust Ned. Cass has never mixed business with pleasure but Dallas is too good and too sexy to remain just a professional colleague. They become colleagues in the bedroom as well as the boardroom, pledging a lifelong commitment to each other. Author Linda Cajio has done it again with a sophisticated and sexy love story.

(continued)